# FILTHY COMMITMENTS

---

A SUBMISSIVES' SECRETS NOVEL 4

MICHELLE LOVE

HOT AND STEAMY ROMANCE

# CONTENTS

Made in "The United States" by:

Michelle Love



ISBN: 978-1-64808-835-3



❀ Created with Vellum

## BLURB

**He needs a fake wife for two weddings, a week-long family vacation, and his high school reunion. A three-month, summer long contract with a sub who is willing to do anything for her Dom should do the trick…**

22-year-old virgin, Asia Jones, should be graduating from Rutgers University in Newark, New Jersey as a Statistical Analyst, but she's failed a couple of classes, ending her scholarships, and making her go out of her comfort zone to get enough money to finish her last year of school.

Jett Simons, is the heir to the 'Cinnamon Buns' global sweet shop. He's young, 26-years-old, and arrogant. He's also a three-year member of 'The Dungeon of Decorum' and he's looking to buy a woman at auction who looks like she needs a strong hand to mold her into the woman she could be. As an added bonus, the lucky chic gets to pretend she's his wife for a few social functions he has throughout the summer.

Using the club's website to browse for a suitable sub, Jett finds the profile of Asia. Not only is she gorgeous, but she's a college student, meaning she must be smart, and the cherry on top is she still has her cherry. He's found himself a good girl to take to occasions he has lined up. Pretty, smart, and virtuous means he's got it made in the shade with this choice.

Or does it?

Jett's main mistake is taking Asia on as his sub before he tells her about the fake marriage. She's not accustomed to lying. When he shows her the list of rules he made out and she accepted, number seven is, she must do as he says at all times, that includes being whoever he asks her to be. A rule she didn't look at close enough. She's stuck, but she's not happy about that part of the contract.

Their time as Dom and sub in his Portland mansion teaches her things about her body she finds amazing. Their time as husband and wife teach them both more about what it means to make marital sacrifices.

Will the fake marriage be a thing that brings them closer or will it break their bond at the end of summer and when their contract is up?

# 1

# JETT

"I don't need your help to find a wife, Mom!" Getting out of my comfortable office chair, I strode over to the windows that ran from floor to ceiling. The sun was setting over the Pacific, creating colors on the water as only the sun can. "I'm not even looking for one. I am only twenty-eight."

"By the time I was your age I was married, I'd had you, and was developing the recipe for the cinnamon buns that got us all where we are today." Her voice had taken on a nasal tone as she bitched at me. "Your father would like to retire someday. A thing he can't do until you're ready to take over the CEO position. This is a family business, Jett. You're our only heir. And you'll need an heir of your own in the future. Don't let all that your father and I worked so hard for go to waste."

And there was the guilt!

Always with the guilt. My mother was a master at wielding it like a double edged sword. She'd inherited it, honestly, her mother used it like a weapon too.

"Mom, can you get to why you called? It's after five, everyone else has gone home for the day, and I'd like to get the hell out of here too." I leaned my shoulder against the wall and sighed, wishing I could just hang up the damn phone. But it was my mother on the end of the line, no one hangs up on their mother!

"Oh, yes dear. I completely forgot to get to that. First, how's it going in L.A.? Is business good? I hope you have those numbers up. After going global last year, we have to uphold those sales figures. We put you in charge of our largest distribution office for a reason. To get your executive feet wet after college. Which you graduated from six years ago, by the way. I thought you'd be at the top by now, giving your old dad a much-needed break. That man peddled my baked goods all over the United States for three years before we made a name for ourselves."

"Mom!" I pinched my brow as she was making my head begin to ache. "I get it. And our sales are great. Now, can you please get to the point of why you called? Surely, it wasn't just to lecture me on how hard you and Dad worked to make Sin-a-buns Sweetshop the successful business that it is."

"Oh, yes! The vacation! The whole family, your grandparents from both sides, Uncle Pete and Aunt Sally, their twins, and everyone else will be at our summer place in the Hamptons during the second week of June. It's like a reunion of sorts, only a really long one. And I've invited a few of the neighbors to stop by for our evening meals. Hopefully, you'll like some of the eligible young women who'll be coming over for the extravagant meals I've planned for each night that week. Maybe find one who suits you and marry her and give me some grandchildren."

"Kind of getting ahead of yourself, aren't you, Mom?"

"Not at all. You need to find a woman, Jett. I mean it. You know you'll have to be married, and all settled down before your father hands over the keys to the company, so to speak. Living like a rock star, the way you've been doing, won't cut it."

Shoving my fist in my pocket, I made my way back to my chair. I wasn't happy about a family gathering that would last an entire week. Topping it off with my mother playing matchmaker for me and all the snooty rich bitches from the Hamptons was the icing on top of a cake that was making me sick to my stomach. "I hardly live like a rock star, Mom."

"What would you call it, Jett? You haven't had a steady girl since high school. You broke little Sandy Smith's heart when you dumped her and went away to college. I saw her mother last week when I went to see your grandmother in New Jersey. She said Sandy and her husband Dave moved to the street we used to live on. Only three doors down from our old house where you two used to sit on the porch swing, holding hands. She was such a sweet girl, Jett. What happened?"

That sweet girl wasn't what she seemed to be. Sandy Smith was the biggest manipulator I'd ever met. Not even eighteen yet and she wanted to get married. She wanted it so badly, she tried to get her ass pregnant to trap me. Lucky for me, I noticed the box of condoms had been messed with and found the pin holes she'd stabbed through the foil pouches. She was quite the bitch.

"We just weren't as compatible as we seemed to be, Mom. Anyway, how's Grandma doing?"

"She's just fine. Her gout was flaring up, so I took her some homemade soup. The trip from Manhattan to Jersey was a bit rough for me, though."

"And how's that? Didn't you let Stan drive you? That is what he's paid to do you know." I spun around in my chair, glancing at the now dark window and wishing I could get off the phone. "Mom, can I call you from my cell?"

"No, I hate those things. I like land lines. You know that, Jett. Anyway, Stan had a doctor's appointment, and I took the car. It's been so long since I've driven myself that I found it difficult to navigate my way back to where we lived for twenty years. And I got melancholy about our simple life in Jersey. I mean, I love our Manhattan penthouse. I love the money that came from all of our hard work too. But it's just such a difference, and I only seem to notice it when I go back there."

"Then don't go." I leaned back in the chair, sure that she was going to make me stay at the office all night just to talk to her.

"My parents live there, Jett. And your father's too. I can't just not go."

"I don't go there. Send the car to pick them up and bring them to you. There, I've fixed your problem. And, Mom, don't go trying to drive yourself around. Let Stan do it. I bet Dad didn't know you took off like that, did he?"

"Well, no. And he was upset with me when I got home and he saw me getting out of the car. He gave me what for, especially when I told him how I had gotten lost twice."

Rubbing the back of my neck, I felt my father's pain. The woman was a genius in the kitchen. In other aspects, not so much. "I love you, Mom. That's why I'll say it one more time, let Stan drive you where you need to go. If he's got an appointment, you can wait. Grandma's gout won't get any better or worse if she gets your soup a few hours later."

"Maybe you're right. Anyway, about finding you a wife, I talked to Gertrude the other day. We were talking about some of the things we could do during the family vacation. Well, she told me that Mrs. Finkerstein's granddaughter will be staying the summer with her. Now, that family is like Hamptons royalty, as you well know. I think that girl might be perfect for you."

And there we were, back to the matchmaking. "Mom, you don't even know her. How could you possibly think she'd be perfect for me? I think you just want to get me in with some snooty family so you can claim to be part of it. Not cool, Mom."

"What's wrong with wanting to belong to a prestigious group? And what's wrong with wanting to see my one and only child happily married? I'm going to push this, Jett. I am!"

I could see that she was. My wheels began to spin. How could I get her off my back?

Lie, of course!

"Mom, I actually have been seeing someone."

"No!"

"Yes. She's actually taken me completely by surprise and, well, dare I say it? I'm head over heels in love, Mom!" The burden of the lie wasn't as heavy as I thought it'd be.

"Jett, why didn't you tell me this from the start? I wouldn't have gone on so long about finding you a suitable wife. Now, tell me all about her. Is she pretty?"

"Gorgeous."

"Is she nice?"

"The sweetest girl I've ever met."

"What's her name? Can you send me a picture of you two? When will we get to meet her? Will you be bringing her to our vacation?"

"I'm not saying another thing about her. You'll just have to be surprised. Who knows, I may be bringing her to meet you as my wife."

"Oh, Jett! I'm so happy!"

So, Mom was off my back, but now who was I going to get to play the part of my gorgeous, sweet wife?

# 2

# ASIA

The big fat F stared back at me as my eyes glossed over. That was the third test I'd failed in my Data Extraction class. One more failed test and I'd have to repeat the class. And that would cost me, dearly.

I had one other class that was giving me fits. I knew I'd fail that one too if I couldn't wrap my head around the concept of statistical models. I had no idea becoming a Statistics Analyst would be so damn hard!

High school had been a breeze for me. I'd sailed through it with nothing but high A's. I was awarded a full scholarship to Rutgers University in New Brunswick, New Jersey. It wasn't too far away from my home in Queens, New York, but far enough away that I got to practice being an adult.

There were stiff stipulations to the scholarship, though. Fail a class, and I would lose it. The whole thing. It paid for my classes, books, dorm room and all my meals on campus. If I lost that scholarship, I'd lose everything. And I had one more year of school to get through. All would've been wasted.

Since I had everything covered, I didn't have a job, not even a part-time one that I could maybe get more hours at during the summer to build up some money to be able to take those classes over again, plus the others I'd need to graduate.

My parents didn't have much, but maybe they could pull it together to help me out. I'd come too far to just quit. I made a call to my mother to feel her out about some financial help. "Hi, Mom. How's it going?"

She made a long, drawn out sigh that already told me things weren't going well. "Your father was laid off yesterday. After fifteen years as a delivery driver, they up and cut him in the first round of layoffs. Can you believe that, Asia? Now, he and I will have to get by on what I make as an administrative assistant at the law office."

So, they were out!

"That's terrible news. How's Dad taking it?" I wadded up the failed test and threw it in the wastebasket. Then I slumped my way to lay on my bed in the dorm I shared with my roommate, Stacy.

"You know your dad, he's taking it hard. He sees it as something personal, which I've told him it isn't. He's one of their highest paid workers. Of course, the company has to get rid of the employees who are paid the most. It's just finances."

"Poor Dad. And how are my sisters? I haven't had time to call them with all the end of the semester testing."

"Spring is about to pop. She and Max are super excited that their first born is almost here. You'll have to try to make it to see her after she has the baby, Asia. I know South Dakota is a ways from here, but she's your sister, and she's worth it."

"I'll do my best." I had no idea how I'd be able to get my ass to South Dakota with no money, but I wasn't about to burden my mother with that.

"Rainbow and Stewart took their brood of three and moved to Alaska. How crazy is that?"

I huffed and rolled over. My sisters were living their dreams as I was failing mine. "That's pretty crazy. What made them want to leave Washington to go way up there?"

"Stewart got a job as a park ranger in some park in Alaska, so they up and moved. Bow says the kids are happy. She's going to homeschool them because they live in the middle of nowhere."

"Damn, she's brave."

"I know! And how about you, my baby girl?"

I wasn't about to let it all out. No matter how bad I felt, I couldn't do that to her. "Me? Oh, I'm fine. I'm getting a job this summer."

"Oh, yeah, what kind?"

I drummed my fingers on the yellow pillow cover as I conjured up a job. "Um, it's a job in retail. I mean, I don't have it yet. I have classes to finish, but once I'm free, then I should get the job."

"Only one more year of school too. I bet you're getting all types of excited about that. Next year will be your last!"

This would be my last year if I couldn't come up with a way to make about ten thousand dollars. Again, Mom didn't need to be bothered with that. "Yep. I am all types of excited alright."

"So, what are your plans, Asia? Where will you be once you've accomplished your goal of a Master's degree?"

"I guess I'll get a job in New York. That's always been what I thought I'd do. I have to do a year of interning next year. Maybe the company that hires me on will keep me."

I had no idea how I'd do a year of intern work. That paid next to nothing. I'd have to do that, take classes, and take on a part-time job somewhere in between it all.

How was I going to do all that?

It was hopeless. I'd never be able to do it all. And even if I could, I doubted there would be enough money to pay for classes, books, and the dorm room. I was fucked!

It was then that I had to contemplate for the first time that I'd end up just like my parents. Uneducated and living by the skin of my teeth. A chill ran through me.

I had to find a way to pay for school. My parents were in their fifties. Dad had lost his job and chances were, at his age, he'd have hell finding another one. And if he did, it wouldn't pay nearly as much as he was making at the job he'd had for years.

"New York is so expensive to live in, Asia. You should think about coming back to Queens. I'm sure you could commute. Maybe live here with your father and me for a while. You could help out with the bills. I don't think your father is going to get another job that pays as well as the one he's lost."

And there it was. They needed me. Guilt piled up on me like a ton of bricks.

"Yeah, I could do that, Mom. You can count on me. I'll figure it all out. I will. You and Dad took good care of us all, I can help you out when I get a good job after I graduate. You'll have to hold out until then, but I'll be there for you guys. I promise."

The sigh of relief she made had my heart hurting. My parents were in dire straits. Any savings they had would run out, and they'd be left living on crumbs. I had to make it all work out. There were no other choices. I'd do whatever I had to.

"You have no idea how good that is to hear, Asia. I'd never ask this of you if I had any other choice. I'm going to tell my boss that I need a raise and we'll get rid of any bills we can. I don't want you to have to live with us forever. The house will be paid off in five years. If you can live with us and help us until that bill is gone, then we'll be fine after that."

Five years!

I couldn't let her know how much that affected me. "I can do that, Mom."

"You're such a good girl, Asia. I know I've told you that a million times, but I have to say it again. You're good as gold. Always such a good girl and my little helper. I don't know what we'd do without you. Your sisters have their own lives and families, I could never ask them for anything. But you're alone and will have a great paying job in just a bit over a year. We can make it until then. We have enough in savings to do that."

"I'm glad I can help. So, let me get off here and check out the internet to start searching for a summer job."

"Hold on. Why do you suddenly need a job? I mean, your scholarship pays for everything."

She finally caught on that things weren't exactly alright with me. "I might have to pay some, that's all. Don't worry."

"Why would you have to pay some all of a sudden?"

I was squirming for an answer when one came to me. "Extra classes that the scholarship won't cover. I want to take a few extra classes."

"Oh," she sounded relieved. "For a moment there I thought you were having some problems of your own. You'd tell me if you were, right?"

With all the shit she had on her, why would I do a thing like that?

"Sure, I would, Mom. I gotta go. Love you."

"Love you. Talk to you soon."

I ended the call and buried my face in the pillow. I was up shit creek without a paddle, as my granddad used to say. With no clue of how I was going to make it all work, I did what any girl does. I started to cry.

# 3

# JETT

Sipping a cold beer as I sat on the deck of my Malibu beach house, I got a message from a guy I went to high school with back in Maplewood, New Jersey. Hot on the heels of my mother's news of a huge family vacation came the news that our high school was having our ten-year reunion on July twenty-fifth at the gym.

Josh was one of my best buddies back in the old days. He was already married with two kids, and anytime I talked to him, his wife was shouting out female names. She wanted to pair me up with one of her single women friends so we could all pal around together. I, of course, wasn't into it.

In college, I messed around with a few different women, not a ton of them. I wasn't quite the playboy my family thought I was. When I turned twenty-five, a friend of mine took me to an exclusive club in Portland, Oregon. He told me I'd find women there that would be more my speed.

Ron and I went out with a couple of women we met at a bar one night. He noticed the way I treated the one I was with. I had certain expectations that she couldn't seem to comply with.

Yappy broads are a thing I couldn't stand. I liked quiet women, who spoke only when they had something interesting to say. Small talk bored me. I liked intelligent women who didn't mind letting me take charge. That's a hard combination to find.

I didn't consider myself bossy or controlling. I thought of myself as a self-assured man who knew what he wanted and how he liked things to be. Not that the world should revolve around me or anything like that. It's just that I didn't like to explain every little thing I did or wanted to a woman. And that had me being single. Not many women want that in a man. But at that club, many, many women did want that.

The Dungeon of Decorum was a dream come true for me. I had taken on three different subs at different times. I also dabbled with quite a few of the women in the club, without making them mine. It was easy to let all of them go. Nothing was ever overly emotional, a thing I liked about the entire setup.

With my subs, there were contracts made that had my rules in them. The women understood what I wanted and complied with everything. I wasn't into any kinks at that time. Normal sex was all I wanted. Mostly, I wanted control. I wanted a woman who did as I told her to. She kept quiet, did anything I asked of her without so much as an eye roll, and laid down for me when I wanted her to. Simple and easy.

After a while, I added in a few things. I found I liked to bind their hands behind their back or over their heads. I liked to cuff them to the bed. And on occasion, I liked to spank them with my hand or a paddle. Nothing overly painful. To me, I'd have to get too into their heads to know what they wanted or needed. I wasn't a typical Dom. I didn't eat and breathe the role as a lot of the men I knew at the club did.

Part of the pleasure they got out of it all was thinking about their sub and what they could do for her. I just wasn't that into it. I wanted that lifestyle for me, not anyone else. Did that make me selfish? Hell yes it did. I didn't care, though. I wasn't in it to make life-long friends. I had a lot of those already.

When Josh's wife started naming off the women she knew that I could take to the reunion, I added to my lie. I told Josh I'd gotten married since we'd talked last. It would be her I'd take to the reunion, he could tell his wife to forget about setting me up any longer.

Now I had two functions I needed a wife for during that summer. A few days later, I received an invitation in the mail from my college roommate. He was getting married on the third Saturday in June. I hated to go to weddings alone. It was just too depressing, and all the bridesmaids hit on me.

I didn't enjoy being hit on. I was the hunter, not the prey.

And as I sat on the deck, finishing off my beer, I got a text from my cousin back in New York. She was getting married at the end of August and wanted me to be there.

Two weddings, a reunion, and a week-long vacation with my extended family and Hamptons' royals. What was I to do?

Not one of the subs I'd ever had was the right kind of woman to play that part. They were all a bit on the nasty and sinister side. I needed a good girl. One you'd find in the house next door. But she'd have to be easy for me to get along with for three months. We'd have to live together to make it all look real.

I had rings to buy. A home in New York would be a great prop too, I thought. I could easily put that all together in no time at all. The only thing I couldn't figure out was how to get a good girl to become my fake wife.

The doorbell rang, and I went through the house to answer it. My neighbor was standing there with a chocolate cake in her hand. "Hey there, handsome."

"Maggie. What's with the cake?" I stepped back to let her in and went to the kitchen to grab another beer. I didn't bother to get her one. She wouldn't be staying.

"I made it for you. Isn't today your birthday, Jett?"

"Nope." I opened the beer and took a long drink. Maggie always had some excuse for why she was coming to my home. I wasn't surprised she'd come up with that one.

She placed the cake, that was caved in on one side, on the dining room table and put her hand on her round hip as she threw her stringy black hair behind her shoulder. "Oh, my bad." Her finger touched her lower lip as she made a vain attempt at looking sexy. "Well, you can have the cake, anyway. Got an extra beer in there, Jett?"

"Nope." I tossed the bottle top into the trash and went back out onto the deck. "Thanks for the cake. You know your way out."

She followed along behind me anyway. "I didn't see any take-out boxes in your trash. Have you eaten dinner yet?"

"I have not. I may call in." Pulling my shades off my head, I put them on and looked out at the ocean, instead of at her.

Maggie annoyed me. She always had. It was just that she was so damn obvious. She wanted me. And that, in itself, turned me off.

I knew to what lengths women would go to who wanted me. I wasn't about to get trapped by any of the conniving bitches.

That's why I liked the whole system of the Dom/sub relationship. If I said to take birth control, they did. If I said don't get your ass pregnant, they obeyed me. Maggie and other women like her couldn't be trusted.

When Maggie walked up to lean on the railing of the deck, she leaned way over as if she was looking at how high up she was. She was showing me her ass. Her large ass that was clad in some short shorts. Funny how it didn't tempt me at all. Not one little bit.

"I could make dinner for you. I make a mean spaghetti." She turned around slow and easy, jutting out her plump breasts. Again, it gave me no rise. She just wasn't the package I wanted.

"If I told you that you were wasting your time on me, would that stop this torture?" I took another drink and looked past her, instead of at her.

"Torture? You think a woman offering you cake and dinner is torture?"

"You're offering me more than that." I pulled my shades down to look over them at her. "If I told you to go to my bedroom. Put on the blindfold that's in the left-hand nightstand drawer. Get naked and on your knees and wait for me, what would your answer be?"

"Which door goes to your bedroom?" She smiled a sinister smile.

"And that is why I don't want you. You're too damn easy, Maggie."

"I'm not into games." She took a few steps, shaking her ass as she went.

"You are into games. I'm not. I'm into straightforward sex with no strings."

"I can do that." She blew a kiss at me.

I took another drink. She was already boring me. "You're not the right one, Maggie. You don't have what I need. I need a good girl."

"I can be your good girl, Jett. Try me."

I got up and took her by the hand, leading her into the house. She was already breathing heavy as I went through the house. Then I opened the front door. "Bye, Maggie."

She stopped the heavy breathing with one loud huff. "Jett Simmons, you're a fucking dick!"

"I know." I closed the door in her face and locked it. Then went back out to my deck to think about what I could do about getting myself a fake wife.

# 4

# ASIA

"Miss Jones, it looks like I'll be seeing you again next semester." Professor Laughton placed the sheet of paper face down on my desk.

I didn't even have to look at it. But the man could bet I wouldn't be taking his class again. I'd find another Data Extracting teacher for my next round with the tougher than hell class.

That also signaled the end of my free ride to college. My scholarship had gone down the drain, and I was left with no idea how to come up with enough money to pay next year's tuition.

My head hung low as I made my way back to the dorms. At least I'd have a roof over my head and food to eat until school got out in a couple of weeks. Bummed didn't even come close to what I was feeling.

Someone bumped shoulders with me, taking my attention from the green grass I was crushing with each footstep. "I've seen better faces on a potato." It was a friend of mine, Joy. She was one of those beautiful rich girls who have no problems. She'd never understand mine. "So, what's up with it?"

"Nothing." I plodded along, trying to get into my room before I burst into tears.

She got in front of me, stopping me and taking my chin in her hand.

Her nails were perfectly manicured with a shiny pink polish on them. Her hair, perfectly quaffed. She was just too perfect. “Something’s wrong. Come on, tell me, Asia. No reason to keep it all bottled up.”

The tears were stinging my eyes. “I’m about to cry, Joy. Just let me go.”

Wrapping her arm around me, I noticed the delicate scent of her perfume. It smelled expensive. “You come with me. I’m not about to leave you to cry alone.” She whisked me away before I could protest.

The next thing I knew, we were sitting in her apartment. She was making margaritas and plating up some chips and salsa. I was soon drowning my sorrows as I ate spicy food. But I still wasn’t feeling any better about things.

Taking a seat at the table across from me, Joy was ready to hear my pitiful story. “Spill it, Asia. All of it.”

The words spilled out of my mouth as tears spilled out of my eyes, “I can’t finish college! I failed a class, and my scholarship is going to get revoked! I have to make a shit-ton of money to pay for everything now, and I don’t know how I’m going to do it!” I bellowed and whined then laid my head on the table and gave up.

“Oh, that’s an easy fix. You can do what I did. I didn’t have any money for college, and I found a way to pay for that and then some.” Her words were crazy. She made no sense to me.

She didn’t have money for college?

The girl reeked of expensive things. She had all the latest styles in clothes. A great car. The bad ass apartment. She had it all and was going to school.

“How?” That’s all I could say as I wiped my eyes and shook my head in disbelief.

Did she really have a great way to make all the money I needed?

“There’s this place in Oregon…”

I cut her off. “I can’t get there. I don’t have money to do that.” It was hopeless. I’d never get to finish school.

“Listen to me, Asia. I signed up for an auction. I put myself up to be a man’s submissive partner. The one I was in was for a two-month contract. The club pays for the plane ticket to get you there. They dress you in their clothes, and when a man purchases you, they take over everything else. They provide you with clothing, food, drink, shelter. You are theirs to take care of for whatever time the contract says."

"That sounds a little bit too good to be true, Joy." I just wasn't believing her. It couldn't be real.

"Well, there are things you must do, of course."

I picked up a napkin and blew my nose. "Of course." I knew it was too good to be true!

"You have to do whatever he wants. But you have control over it all."

"That's an oxymoron if I ever heard one. Do what he wants, yet I'm in control." I wasn't buying it.

"Yes, you see you fill out a list of things you will and won't do. For instance, I won't ever do knife or gun play."

"Fuck! What kinds of shit do these men want?" I was shocked.

"It's BDSM, Asia. I know you've heard about it. Who hasn't?" She took a little sip of the margarita and looked up as if I was a fool.

"BDSM? The hitting stuff? The tying up stuff? The men dominating women stuff?" I shook my head the whole time and wondered what kind of females sign themselves up for that.

A wry grin curled her lips. "Oh, you'd be shocked how great it all feels. You go to another place and time when you're doing it. And this club makes sure the Doms are well-trained. There's nothing to worry about. You learn so much about your mind and body, and you get paid to do it. It's a win-win."

"More like a lose-lose. You're talking about selling your body, Joy." I was feeling a bit sick to my stomach. My friend wasn't who I thought she was at all!

"If it's that, then why did I never feel that way. Hell, I felt like I was getting paid to feel pleasure beyond my wildest dreams. The things that were done to me, I'd have gladly paid someone to do. It was that good, Asia."

Somehow I was becoming more intrigued than disgusted. "And how will I be in control?"

"The safeword and the fact there will be no kind of play that you don't previously approve of. The talking about what you'll do is almost as enticing as the doing it part." She licked her lips and closed her eyes. "And you'll have those memories forever! Sometimes, I can still hear my Dom telling me to sit still, or he'll spank my ass. Then I'd wiggle just to get him to do it. It'd make me wet and horny every single time."

I was back to being disgusted. "There's something wrong with you, Joy."

"If that's true, then I'm cool with that. And I'm not the only one, either. There were hundreds of women at the club. Not all were in the auction. Some were there to be pleasured by the men without accepting any form of payment for it."

"So why pay for a sub at an auction if they can have women who will do it for free?"

"Because some men want it to last longer than one session. Some want to take the girl with them. Some want to keep her for a while. Believe me, once you've been kept, you will know the true meaning of power. You'll give yours and get theirs. It's an exchange that will change you forever."

Joy had never talked about any man in her life, it had me curious. "Did you fall in love with the man who bought you?"

"Love?" She shook her head. "No. Not love. I respected him immensely. I loved the way he made me feel. But I didn't love him. To be honest, he kept his guard up, not ever completely letting me in. I was fine with that. And I was ready for it to end. The intensity can get overwhelming."

"Would I have to be in an auction? Because I don't want to be with a man I've never seen. I'd like to pick. Or is that impossible?" I couldn't believe what I was saying.

Was I going to do this?

"You can sign up as available for a contract. You'll have to have a physical which the club will pay for. Then you'll pick out the kinds of play you will and won't do. If you get an interested man, he'll message you, I think. It's different than the auctions. But you will have the choice of telling him yes or no."

"So I could hold out for a man who I feel attracted to?"

"You could." She took out her phone and pulled up the site. "The Dungeon of Decorum is like something out of a fantasy book. It's like a dream you never knew you wanted to have."

My wheels were spinning. I could do it. I could be in some control. And I had a secret too. Something that might just get me more money than most. I was a virgin.

There was one more thing I had to know. "Joy, how much money were you paid for the two months?"

"Two hundred and fifty thousand dollars."

"Fuck me!"

I was in!

# 5

# JETT

The end of May was looming just around the corner. My family's vacation was getting close, and I had to come up with a bride, and fast!

No one in my immediate circle would do. I had to venture out, and even then I found no one that I thought I could get along with for three months.

Then it came to me that I could search The Dungeon of Decorum's website for a prospect. I was short on time, I had nowhere else to look.

With my fingers crossed, I pulled up the website and began to browse. Unfortunately, the women who were into the BDSM scene were mostly going for that classic bad girl look. I didn't want a bad girl, I wanted a good one.

Just as I was about to give up hope, I saw her. Asia Jones was her name, and she looked like an angel. And she had to be smart too. She was in college at Rutgers, majoring in statistics. A little boring but she had to be damn smart to want to do that.

I ran my fingertips over her pink cheek on the computer screen. Her hair hung in a silky sheet of black hair that looked as it if went to her waist it was so long. Her bangs were long, framing her beautiful face.

Almond shaped eyes with doe-like brown irises looked peaceful as thick dark lashes surrounded them. Her skin was the color of coffee with a lot of cream in it. Her lips were pink and just the right amount of plump. High cheekbones made her look just a touch on the exotic side. She was a real beauty.

She was the one!

But there was her list to get through. She allowed spanking, different types of sensory deprivation was a thing she would do. Bondage would be okay with her. Those were all I really cared about.

My cell rang, and I saw my mother was calling. "Hi, Mom."

"Jett, I can't wait to meet her. You two are still together, right?"

"We sure are. And boy are you going to be surprised." I smiled at Asia's picture. Mom would adore her.

"I want to know her name. I need to make place settings." Her way of getting it out of me, but it wasn't going to work.

"You can put Mrs. Jett Simmons on her name card. She'll get a kick out of that, I bet." Would Asia get a kick out of being called Mrs. Simmons? Would she like being called my wife?

"Oh, my! Are you really going to marry her before you get here, Jett?" Mom was on a level I'd never heard before. Excitement, mixed with high octane adrenaline filled her voice.

"I am, Mom. I'm going to do it." If Asia would agree to be mine.

I would have to make sure the pot was sweet enough to get her to jump right in with both feet. I'd bought a house in a ritzy suburb outside of New York. I'd let her have it if she played nicely with me.

"I wish you'd get married here, son. Your father and I'd love to be with you on your special day. Please tell me you'll think about it." Her whimpering was tearing at my heartstrings.

But there would be no real wedding for her to attend. "Sorry, Mom. Asia wants it to be just the two of us. She's shy. You understand, don't you?"

"Shy?" She seemed confused. "Who's so shy they don't want a proper wedding?"

"Already finding fault with my beloved, Mother?" I used my stern tone with her. I didn't want her to bother Asia with her silly notions of what was proper and what wasn't.

I chuckled at how I was already thinking in terms that the woman on the computer screen would soon be with me, playing the part of my wife. While really she'd be my sub.

I'd never made a woman be something she wasn't before. It was new to me, and I was pretty sure it'd be new to Asia too. Would she mind it? Should I tell her about the fake marriage up front?

I thought that might be better left until after the contract was signed. I could word it in such a way she'd have no choice. That's what I'd do!

"Goodness, no. If she's shy, that's fine. I'll give her time to get to know me. She and I will be best friends!"

My mother and sub, best friends!

I had to chuckle again. "I'm sure you will."

"You sound so happy, Jett. She makes you happy, doesn't she?"

"Yes, she does." I ran my fingers over the screen and wished it was her I was touching. "She's lovely, Mother. The kind of girl you've always wanted for me. Smart, beautiful, and down to Earth. I can't wait for you guys to meet her."

I knew I was asking for a miracle that Asia could be all those things. But I wanted it all to be true. I wanted her to be the woman I thought would be perfect for me.

It was the oddest thing when I looked at that picture. I could see her in a way I'd never seen anyone. It was if I had seen her before. Like maybe in my dreams. She seemed so familiar, so right.

"I'm so happy. I'll let you go. I've got place cards to order with my daughter-in-law's name on them. Love you."

"Love you, Mom."

I put the cell down and scrolled down to read more about the woman who was intriguing me so. She was a little thing at 5 feet 3 inches. Her hometown was Queens. Her hobbies were hiking, which I liked too and row boating, which I hadn't done, but thought it sounded cool. Looking at what she was wearing, I liked her style. A crisp white shirt with a lace collar looked cute on her. She was demure, yet captivating. She'd make a great mom. I could see her putting kids on a bus or driving them to school, shouting 'I love you' as they walked away from her. She'd smile and get back into the car, looking like a little doll who was all mine.

Then it hit me that I was thinking like a fool. I was pretending she could be what I really wanted. She'd be my sub. She'd do as I told her to, pretend to be my wife and anything else I said.

I didn't know why I was being so ridiculous. It was as if her picture alone stirred something inside me. But I knew she'd be like all the other subs I'd had. She was there to make money, I was sure. She wasn't the type to be there because she actually wanted to be there. I'd had two subs who needed money, and that's why they came to the Dungeon. Women who did it because they wanted to were much better to work with. They enjoyed it when I spoke sternly to them. Ruled them with an iron fist. Asia needed money, I was certain of that.

But she'd look the part, and if she wanted my money, she'd act it too!

I scrolled down some more, and the words that popped up made my cock thump.

My little Asia was a virgin!

## 6

# ASIA

The message light was blinking on my laptop as I opened it. The Dungeon of Decorum had an app I'd downloaded onto the desktop. I was sure it was a message from the woman named Isabel who I'd spoken with. She made the arrangements for my physical examination and sent me a message when the results were sent to her. I was sexually healthy, physically healthy, and the doc confirmed my birth control method of the pill and had given me six more months of them.

She told me, she'd send me a message as soon as my profile went up on the website. That's what I thought I'd find when I opened the app. And there was one message from her, but also one from a man named Jett Simmons.

Did I have my first nibble?

I opened Isabel's message, and it was just as I expected, a welcome letter. Then I opened the one from the Dom who was interested in me. My heart was pounding just as hard as if I was about to meet him in person.

The message was short and to the point. I like the looks of your profile. Let's talk.

I typed back that I'd love to talk to him and I'd also love to have his profile since he'd seen mine. The reply was instantaneous. And I was looking at his handsome face as my jaw hung open. There may have been a tad bit of spittle hanging from my lower lip as I was salivating like a Saint Bernard over the man.

His hair was shoulder length, chocolate brown with golden tones and highlights that hung in luscious waves. His skin was tanned, and his features were chiseled. His description said he was 6'3" and he was built like a beast. The black suit he wore hugged his biceps, making them stand out. Sea green eyes surrounded by dark lashes looked daunting, commanding. He looked like a Dom. His kinks were bondage, minor impact play such as spanking and paddling, sensory deprivations such as blindfolds, complete darkness, music so loud you can't hear yourself think, and fantasy play.

He didn't sound bad at all. And I had to admit that I found him extremely attractive. I could be his sub. But for how long would he want me? And more importantly, what would he pay?

Another message popped up. It was his phone number. I just thought my heart was pounding when I looked at his message, now it was almost exploding out of my chest. He wanted me to call him!

My fingers were shaking as I called the number. "Asia?"

"Jett?"

"Hi. I'm glad you called. I'm not a message back and forth type of man," his voice was deep, smooth, and it relaxed me right away.

"Me neither. I prefer to speak my words, rather than write them." I took a deep breath to further calm my nerves.

"Do you mind telling me what you need the money for, Asia?"

"College. I've never had trouble with any of my classes before. I was given a full scholarship to Rutgers. But a couple of classes have kicked my tail-end this year. I failed them, and it ended the free ride I was given. With one more year to go, I need money, or I'll be forced to quit school."

"That's a reasonable reason to need money. Will you be available for the months of June, July, and August?"

"Yes, sir." My stomach was gurgling as I thought we were getting close to making a commitment to one another.

"That's excellent. Would you like to hear my offer, Asia?"

"Yes, sir."

He cleared his throat. "My offer is 300,000 dollars, plus a brand new Mercedes, the color will be your choice. There will be some jewelry I'll expect you to wear at all times. You'll get to keep it at the end of the contract. You can sell it or keep it, whichever you prefer. If you're very good, there will be the bonus of the house I've purchased in the Sterling Ridge area of Harrison, New York."

I was on the edge of my seat with all he had offered. Who could offer me any more than all of that?

And he was handsome. Yes, he looked a bit demanding, but what should one expect out of a Dom?

In the vein of it all sounding too good to be true, I had to ask, "Is that a normal amount a man pays for a temporary sub?"

"It's a bit on the high side. It's the highest I've ever paid for a sub, but I think you're special, mainly for the virginity part. I need a nice young woman, and your innocence pleases me immensely. You're gorgeous in an earthy way and will do for what I need. As long as you realize I'm a strict Dom, then things should be fine between us. But I need an answer soon."

I had to ask just one more thing, "Will you be gentle when you take my virginity?"

His reply was quick, "Of course." It settled my nerves even more. My profile had barely been published, and I'd already gotten an offer that was above and beyond any I could've dreamt of. And the man was devastatingly handsome to boot!

"It seems you and I are both in a hurry. And I am impressed with your offer. I do believe I can be what you need, sir."

The way his breath filled my ear through the phone, sent a shiver down my spine and heat through the rest of me. "My God, your voice does something to me, Asia. And your manner pleases me already."

"I must admit the sound of your voice comforts me. I was worried about doing this, but I feel you'll do right by me." Getting out of the chair at my small desk, I spun around as glee filled me.

"You can trust me, Asia. The main thing I want is your respect and your obedience. It's not that hard to please me. Do as I say at all times, be at my beck and call, and above all, be who I want you to be."

I could be the sugar plum fairy for the man for all he was going to give me. Mom and Dad would have nothing to worry about, I could take care of them and me too!

Then it hit me. How would I explain my sudden wealth to them? The house and car would be hard to explain. The money could be hidden in my bank account.

I shrugged it off. I'd deal with that when it came time to. They didn't have to know the deal I was making to get us all out of our financial woes.

"May I ask you where we'll be all summer, sir?"

"In the New York area at the home I told you about. Is that a problem?"

"Not at all. It's fantastic, actually. My parents will want to know where I am. Not that I'm a child and have to answer to them. But it's a common courtesy to let them know where I am. You do understand, don't you, sir?"

"I do. As long as you understand, you are mine for the duration of the contract. You can only go see them if I allow it."

The thought was daunting. I was put off for a moment. I couldn't go see my own parents if I wanted to. And for three whole months?

"Would that be a thing you'd allow, sir?"

"Most likely."

His answer was short and to the point. He was a man of few words, it seemed. Not much on explaining himself about anything. But wasn't that what Joy told me about her Dom?

He hadn't let her in entirely. Maybe that was one of the main traits of men who wanted what they did. Whatever it was, I didn't love that aspect of him.

But not everything he did would please me, just like anyone else. And not all I did would please him. Or would it?

I would have to make sure it would, or I might not get the entire amount. And my lack of sexual knowledge might bore him.

"Mr. Simmons, are you sure my virginity isn't a problem?"

"It's a blessing, Asia. Now, come on. Do you accept my offer or don't you? I'm not a man who waits around."

"I'll do my best to please you, sir. I will accept your offer. Now, what happens?" I was on pins and needles. I was about to be bound to a stranger for an entire three months. And even stranger than that, I was about to have more than I'd ever had or thought possible!

"We'll meet in Portland, Oregon at The Dungeon of Decorum to sign the contract. I'll be in touch as soon as I can make the arrangements. We'll be seeing each other very, very soon. Have a good evening, my little Asia."

"You too, sir."

I put the phone down and fell on my bed. I was a sub! I had a Dom! What the fuck had I done?

# 7

# JETT

For the first time in a very long time, I felt on the edge of giddy. I had her, the one I wanted. Asia Jones would be my sub and fake wife for the next three months!

I pulled the black boxes out of the drawer of my nightstand and looked the wedding set over. The engagement ring was three karats, the wedding bands were platinum, and I was going to give Asia all of the rings that cost thousands of dollars.

Just like any divorced woman, Asia would leave our contract with a huge home, a new car, jewelry that was worth a lot of money, plus a large chunk of cash to call her own. I really was changing the girl's life for the better.

And I'd teach her along the way about the finer things in life. Along with that, she'd get the knowledge of how to be a good sub. If she ever did find herself in need of money again, she'd have something to fall back on.

My heart felt as if someone had pinched it. It was an odd feeling, and it came about when I thought about Asia being some other man's sub. And there it was once more.

Was that jealousy?

I'd never experienced it before. It was hard to tell. And it was unnerving. Asia and I were complete strangers. I shouldn't have any feelings for her at all. Except maybe gratitude. But even that wasn't a thing I should feel towards her. I was paying her for her trouble. As if being with me would be any trouble at all.

I wasn't a monster. As a Dom, I was quite reasonable. And I wasn't hard on the eyes. I knew my way around a woman's body. I could bring pleasure to the little virgin that she'd never dreamt of. Asia would be lucky to have me.

I hoped she'd think so too.

Not wasting a moment, I called Isabel to get her going on the contract. "Isabel, here. How may I help you this evening?"

"This is Jett Simmons, Isabel. I hope you're doing well."

"I am, Mr. Simmons. How nice to hear from you. How can I help you?"

"Asia Jones and I have made an agreement, and I need you to draw up a contract for us. It will be for the months of June, July, and August." I ran my hand through my hair, pushing it back and looking out my bedroom window. The waves were small that evening, lapping at the sandy beach. I wondered if I'd bring Asia to my home in Malibu. Perhaps if she was along the lines of what I expected her to be, I would.

"Asia Jones? My, my. She got scooped up quickly. I just set her up in the system this afternoon."

"You sound surprised by that. I felt I had to hurry to give her an offer she couldn't refuse. I was certain men would be throwing themselves at her." I chuckled as I thought about all the men who'd look at her profile and attempt to contact her. But I'd taken her already. Well, as soon as the contract was signed, she'd be mine.

"I know I shouldn't be surprised at all. Virgins never last long once we get them." Her laughter was shrill as it pierced the air. It was a bit on the witchy side and made a chill run through me.

It made me wonder how Asia really felt about giving her virginity to a man she didn't love or even know for that matter. My heart felt heavy for her. She'd hung onto that longer than most, yet she was ready to sell it, so to speak, to a stranger.

I'd do right by the girl. I promised myself I would. I'd try not to be as closed off as I usually was. I'd try to form at least a bit of a bond. Then her memory of her first time would still be special. I hoped so anyway.

"How soon can you have a contract ready, Isabel?"

"Two days. I have to write it up and get one of the founders to approve it. So what are your rules, Mr. Simmons?"

"I want her to do as I say at all times and be who I want her to be." I thought about how to word the rule so she'd have no choice but to play the part of my wife.

"Well, let's get the general rules out of the way first. Is she to kneel when you enter a room?"

"I don't want that. I want to treat her differently than I treated the others. Not entirely like my sub. I want to give her more respect than that. Do you know what I mean?" I was having a hard time figuring out what I wanted to do with Asia, exactly. "Can we have a broad set of general rules. She can't go anywhere unless I approve. She can't wear anything I haven't given her."

"Will there be any special diet rules or drinking rules?"

"No. I see no reason for that. I'll be in control of that anyway. She'll be with me all the time."

"Will she sleep in her own bedroom?"

"No, we'll share a bed." Any normal married couple shared a bed, so would we.

"How about the forms of play you will be delving into, Mr. Simmons?"

"There will be bondage, sensory deprivation, and spanking with hands and paddles. Nothing more needs to be in the contract. This time around I need full cooperation more so than physical domination."

"So there will be more mental domination then?" Her question bothered me for some reason.

I didn't want to think about mentally harming the young woman. But in the end, what would you call what I wanted to do? I wanted her to do as I said at all times. I supposed it was mental domination. "Yes, it will be more mental than anything else."

That didn't sit well with me. In my opinion, the body was almost a separate entity from the mind. Things happen to our bodies all the time to scar and mar what was once perfect flesh. The skin that's broken is tougher when it heals, making it difficult to re-injure the area. And minds are like that too. Only when there's a scar on it, it changes how a person acts and feels.

I didn't want to mentally damage Asia. But I did plan on making her do what I told her to. And that was the first time I realized that what I was doing would leave its mark on her. If not on her flesh, then on her mind. Her soul, itself.

Our marriage might be fake, but she'd remember me forever. Our time together would be a thing that would shape and mold the future Asia Jones. Suddenly a tremendous amount of responsibility was felt, weighing me down like nothing had before.

It made me wonder if that's what a real marriage felt like. Did one bear the burden of the other through it all? Was that what held marriages together, the combination of responsibility for your partner's physical and mental health and happiness?

Did I care if Asia was happy?

I had never cared if any of the others were. I cared if they were happy with the sex or the type of play we were doing. But did their happiness ever even occur to me?

I couldn't recall a time when it had. But there I was, thinking about the happiness of a girl I'd never met. All I knew about her was that she was as pretty as a picture, and her voice was as sweet as honey. And she was going to be mine.

"It almost sounds as if you're doing a marriage fantasy. Is that what taking this sub is about, Mr. Simmons?"

"Um. Well..." She saw right through it. Would Asia? And if she did, would she still sign the contract? "It's a little like one. I tell you what, throw in kneeling when I enter the room, but only when we're completely alone." That made it sound more like a normal contract. I didn't want to risk Asia backing out on me at the last minute. Not only did I desperately need her as I'd dug myself into a hole with my lies about being married, but I wanted her. I wanted Asia more than I'd ever wanted anyone.

And that was a thing that was beginning to bother me. Was I going to let a woman and my need for her control me?

# 8

# ASIA

From the moment I stepped onto the plane, it was like everything wasn't real. The people on the plane who chattered away. The stewardess who gave us all the speech about what to do if the plane crashed. The man who was sitting next to me who smelled like cabbage and sausages. Nothing seemed real.

Then I seemingly floated off the plane and made my way through the terminal until I found a man who had my name on a sign he was holding. I had one carry-on bag and my purse. I was told I didn't need to bring anything more than my personal products, my birth control and my identification. My Dom would provide everything else for me.

It was like a fairy tale. One where I was the princess who was on her way to meet her prince. We'd marry and have a happily ever after life.

Only that wasn't the case at all. I was to be submissive to a man I didn't know. I was to allow him to do things to my body I'd never let other men do. And all of this was because I needed money.

The root of all evil, indeed!

As I rode in the back of the car that took me to The Dungeon of Decorum, I thought about the man I was going to meet. He and I didn't talk much after our first phone call. It was Isabel who called me and told me about the plans. Jett had given me one call just before I got on the plane.

He said he was excited to be meeting me and he hoped we'd get along well. I assured him we would. I wasn't about to do a single thing to make our time together hard or unhappy for him. I was there to please him and please him I would.

I'd studied up on sexual acts. I'd practiced oral sex on a cucumber. I was sure in my ability to please my Dom. He'd be getting a virgin, but one who'd studied up for him.

I hoped he would like that.

There were so many things I hoped for. I hoped he'd be nice. I hoped he let me in, even if it was just a bit. I hoped he liked me.

That was the biggest fear I had. That he wouldn't like me.

The car pulled off the highway and went out to the very edge of town. We took a turn, and all I saw was a parking garage and a long driveway. As we made our way up it, I began to think things were moving too fast.

In no time I'd be seeing Jett, and things would begin to feel real. Maybe too real!

Panic began to stab me all over my body. Anxiety took me over, and I held my hand over my pounding heart as if that would steady it. My breathing became erratic, and I broke into a sweat.

The car came to a stop, and I tried, desperately to calm myself down. There was a bottle of wine in a chiller, and I opened it and took a long drink. A thing that was so not like me. Just as I was placing it back in the chiller, the driver opened my door. "Miss Jones, we've arrived at our destination."

"Yes, yes, of course, we have!" I shimmed across the long leather seat and grabbed my purse and bag then got out of the car.

There was no building. I half expected to see a castle. Instead, I saw what looked like a small shack with a red door on it. The walkway up to it was long. Each step I took made my heart beat a bit faster.

This was it. I was really going through with it. I was handing my body over to a man for three months for money and things. I stopped mid-stride as my mind spun out of control.

What was I doing? I couldn't possibly do this!

I wasn't this person. I was a strong, smart female with goals and achievements. I wasn't some empty-headed woman who was out to make a quick dime.

If I wasn't that woman, then what the hell was I doing there?

I didn't belong there. I knew I didn't. I wasn't one of them. I was an impostor. I wouldn't be able to please a man the way the rest of the subs could. I'd never live up to any of the other subs Jett Simmons had ever had.

He was a true Dom, in my opinion. Maybe not the kind who enjoys bringing a lot of pain into the situation, but he liked to rule. I could tell it by the tone of his voice and the look in his eye. Even if it was only a snapshot of the man. It was there, buried deep in his sea green eyes. He was the ruler. The supreme master. And I'd be his little love slave. A thing I didn't even know how to be.

My stomach rumbled as my guts twisted with more anxiety than I'd ever experienced. I felt like I might faint. I was breathing all weird as black began to tunnel my vision.

I had to leave. I couldn't go through with it. I just couldn't!

Somewhere in the distance, the sound of a car filtered in. I was standing as still as a stone as I heard it stop and a door opened. "Asia, is that you?"

I turned so slowly. I thought it had to be a dream. I must've passed out and was lying on the cement sidewalk, dreaming about Jett Simmons. Or was it real?

He was wearing an expensive black suit. His golden brown hair was bouncing around his broad shoulders as he made his way to me. Pulling his aviator-style shades away, his green eyes pierced me. A smile curved his chiseled lips. "Asia, it is you."

"Mr. Simmons?" I knew it was him, I just didn't know what the hell else to say.

I was all ready to leave. I was ready to throw in the towel. But as I looked into the shiny depths of his gorgeous eyes, I found peace in them. I found safety in them. I'd be safe with the man. I could tell that then.

"Jett. Call me by my name, please." His strong and muscular arm came around my narrow shoulders, enclosing me in the safest embrace I'd ever felt.

My stomach stopped bubbling. My mind stopped moving so fast. It was as if time was standing still as we looked at one another in person for the first time. He was magnificent. Everything about the man screamed power. I didn't need a contract to do what he told me to. I'd have done it anyway, he exuded that much force.

And what was so odd was that it turned me on in a way I didn't know was possible. My body was full of sharp stabbing pricks of electricity. His hand ran down my arm then he grasped my hand and pulled it to his lips. They were the color of caramel nougat. They looked delicious, and I wondered how long he'd wait to kiss me. I hoped not long. I wanted to taste the man so badly it was insane!

"Jett, yes sir, I'll call you that." He kissed the top of my hand then, and it made my knees weak.

"Good girl. I have to say your natural demeanor impresses me, immensely. Are you ready to get inside and sign the contract?" He nodded toward the red door. "It's just inside and down the stairs. I'd rather not take you all the way into the club. What happens inside that red door is not for innocent eyes, I'm afraid."

"I believe you. I was about to chicken out when you came up."

"Then it's a good thing I arrived when I did, isn't it? Are you okay with it now? You don't want to back out, do you?" He ran the tips of his fingers up my arm, over my shoulder, then to my chin where he held it, gently. His eyes darted back and forth, searching mine. "Because now that I've seen you and touched you, Asia, the hunger I've had has turned ravenous. I'd mourn the loss of what could've been for the rest of my life if you changed your mind about me."

"I want to be yours, Jett," the words slipped off my tongue without any will of my own. I did want to be his. I wanted it more than I'd ever wanted anything.

In a split second, everything had changed, and the smile he gave me made my heart sing. Taking my hand, he led me to the red door. When he took me inside, everything in my life changed.

# 9

# JETT

When my eyes landed on Asia, it was as if time was standing still. She was standing there as if she'd been waiting for me to arrive. She wore a cream-colored, sleeveless dress with two-inch black heels. Her hair moved like ribbons in the gentle breeze. Her natural beauty was enhanced with just enough makeup.

I had to pull my sunglasses away so I could take her in completely. Her lips were stained ruby red, her cheeks a pale pink. Her doe-like eyes took me in from head to toe as she wore an impressed expression. She was quiet as she waited, not shouting and throwing her hands up the way a lot of females did.

Elegance and demure beauty, along with fantastic posture, gave her an air of aristocracy. Like a princess, she waited for her prince to join her. I was far from a prince, a thing she looked like she deserved.

Would she like me?

And why was I caring so damn much about that?

The moment my hand touched her, it felt as if thousands of needles were pricking my skin. I hoped I was playing it cool, not letting her know how much she was affecting me.

Staying in control with her was hard. I wanted to pick her up, toss her over my shoulder and take her right back to the car and devour her.

Her rosebud lips were quivering a bit, and I yearned to kiss the nerves away for her.

I wondered how long I could wait before I kissed her.

How long would I wait before I took her body to heights she couldn't possibly comprehend? How long would I have to wait?

A foot shorter than me, she fit neatly against my side when I hugged her. She admitted to me she'd had second thoughts. I was more than overjoyed that all that doubt seemed to vanish with my presence. She could be what I wanted. I could tell that already.

We made our way into the club where I took her right to Isabel's office to get the contract signed. I couldn't make her mine fast enough!

As we walked down the dark stairwell and into the lighted hallway, I saw one of the club's founders coming out of Isabel's office. "Is that you, Mr. S.?"

"It is." I let go of Asia to shake Grant Jamison's hand. "Asia, this is one of the founders of this prestigious club. You may call him, Mr. J."

Grant took Asia's hand and kissed the top of it. "Asia, it's a pleasure to meet you. I heard you'll be entering into a contract with this man here."

"Yes, sir." Asia's eyes darted to mine then back to his. "You're a founder of The Dungeon of Decorum?"

"I am the primary founding father." Grant glowed with pride as he pushed his hand through his salt and pepper hair.

Asia wore a curious expression. "What made you want to start a business like this?"

Grant and I looked at her with surprise. I didn't expect that out of her and apparently neither did he. But he answered her anyway, "I had a need that wasn't being fulfilled. It's not easy to find partners to do the things we do. One can't simply head out to one of the local taverns and pick up a girl, take her home and string her up then flog her until she's going into another state of mind."

"No, I suppose one can't do that." Asia nodded then looked at me. "You won't string me up, will you?"

I grinned and moved my hand down to her round ass, leaving it there. "I'm not into that kind of play, it's too time-consuming for my tastes. You'll find out what I like, and I've read your list of acceptable kinks, you'll be fine, I promise you that." Her ass fit perfectly in my hand, just like everything else about her was working for me. I was growing impatient and wanted the paperwork out of the way. I wanted Asia alone with me to explore each other more deeply.

Hesitation filled her face, and Grant noticed it. "Miss Jones, this is a thing you want to do, isn't it? I mean, the reason we have this club is to make sure all the members, male and female, are doing things they want to. Have you read up on BDSM at all?"

She shook her head. "No, sir. I thought it best to let my Dom teach me what he wanted me to know."

Moving my hand off her ass to rest it on the small of her back, I whispered, "Great answer. And I'm glad you thought that way."

Grant seemed a bit worried about her as he placed his hand on her shoulder. "We don't want you to do anything you don't want to. If you feel like you've jumped into something that you feel is over your head, please let your Dom know that. He's not out to hurt you in any way." He moved his eyes to mine. "She's not a typical sub. You go easy on her." Then he looked back at Asia. "If you're absolutely positive that's what you want, Miss Jones."

She looked at me then smiled. "It is what I want. I feel safe with him Mr. J., and Isabel told me I can make one phone call if I ever want out of the contract. I'm not worried at all. I want to do this with him. Thank you for your concern, sir."

Nothing she said could've pleased me more. "There you have it, Mr. J. she's ready and willing. And I'll treat her very well, you can rest assured of that."

He clapped me on the back, sending us in to see Isabel to finally make things secure between us. Isabel stood up to greet us, shaking our hands and gesturing for us to take the two leather chairs that were in front of her cherry wood desk. "You two look like you're already getting along well."

"I think we are." I nudged Asia with my shoulder. "How about you?"

Her eyes were soft as she looked at me with only a hint of a smile. "I think we are too."

"That's very good to hear." Isabel pushed the contract toward me first. "Please read this over, Mr. Simmons. I want to be sure I've put everything you wanted into it."

I looked the one-page contract over and saw that it had all I wanted on it. Then I handed it to Asia. "Your turn to read our contract, Asia."

She murmured, "Our contract." I watched her as she read it and nodded. "Yes, this is what he and I have discussed. I agree to it all."

Isabel handed her a pen, and she signed it as I let out the breath I hadn't realized I'd been holding in. Then I signed it too, and we were a done deal.

For the next three months, anyway.

"The money will be held in our bank in an escrow account for you, Miss Jones. If either of you decides you want out of the contract, it will be up to the Dom to decide if you get any of the funds he set aside for you. Do you understand that, Miss Jones?" Isabel moved the financial page to Asia, and she signed it too. Isabel smiled at me. "You've been very generous, Mr. Simmons. I do hope you two find what you're looking for."

I didn't have to hope. I knew I'd found the right woman to play my wife. And she already exhibited signs of being a perfect sub for me. I wasn't sure how I got so lucky, but I felt like I'd won the lottery.

Getting up to leave, I took Asia by the hand and went out to where the car was waiting to take us back to the airport. "Is all the flying bothering you?"

She shook her head. "Not so far. We only have a few hours back to New York, right?"

"I chartered a private jet. It'll be a couple of hours, and in the meantime, we'll enjoy dinner in the air. I've ordered lobster and steaks." I opened the door for her and out we went into the still sunny early evening.

"That's thoughtful of you."

The driver hurried to open the back door of the car to let us in. She slid in, and I took the seat next to her. I gave her some room, although I wanted to be as close to her as I could get.

I wasn't sure when I was going to give her the news about the fake marriage and how I expected her to act about it. She seemed up for anything in a laid back kind of way.

Surely, she wouldn't hate the idea.

Would she?

## 10

# ASIA

Although a sense of calm had washed over me, I began to mull over the things I'd read in the contract I had signed. There was a part about the fact no kidnapping charges could ever be filed on my Dom. I wondered why there had to be a thing like that. Had the man who'd just become my Dom kidnapped someone before?

And then there was the part about me not being able to wear anything other than what he gave me. I had to do as he said at all times too. While those things might seem easy enough to do for the amount of money he was giving me, I wondered if I could do that for three whole months. I wasn't without a brain, I could make my own decisions, and I made good ones. So why would I even need a man to make such small decisions for me?

The answer was easy. I wouldn't!

But this was a role I was playing is how I had to look at it. For three months I'd be this man's puppet. It was a notion I'd have to settle into.

Jett poured a tall glass of Champagne and handed it to me then poured one for himself. Facing me, he gave me a smile. "This may seem silly, but it might not after you hear what I have to say."

I nodded and waited with curiosity. The man was a bit different than

I'd imagined he'd be. I was quickly finding out that I couldn't count on him acting any certain way.

He reached into his pocket and pulled out two small black boxes. He opened one lid, and I saw a thick platinum wedding band in it. He pulled it out and put it on his finger. "You're married?" I was horrified!

"No!" He chuckled. "The look on your face is priceless. No, I'm not married."

He opened the next box, and there was a brilliant diamond engagement ring and a wedding band that matched his. I stared at the opulent rings. "What's this about?"

"Hold out your left hand." His eyes held mine as I did as he said to. He slipped the rings onto my finger, and I felt the weight of them as if it was an ominous sign. "Jett, I don't understand."

The pad of his thumb ran over my finger and the rings he'd placed on it. "I need a fake wife for a few occasions this summer. That's the main reason I purchased you."

"To lie to people?" I was more than a bit shocked. The man who was sitting next to me should never have to purchase a woman. He was drop dead gorgeous, wealthy, and I thought he was charming to boot. Why would he need me to lie about such a thing as being his wife?

"Well, yes." His hand traveled up my arm, leaving heat in its path. "Asia, I have my reasons, and frankly, I don't like explaining myself to others. That's why I decided a sub would be best for this task."

I downed the drink and put the glass down. He followed my lead and drank his up too. "So I can't ask you any questions about anything?" I was beginning to get a little dumbfounded by the man.

He put his empty glass down, next to mine. "No, you can't. That was one of the rules. Don't you recall that?"

"Not one that stated that exactly." I tried to remember all thatwas on that paper. I didn't think I'd seen anything that said I couldn't ask him any questions. "But I can follow that rule. What I'm having trouble with is the lying. Who will I be lying to, exactly?"

"My family, friends, people I went to college and high school with. Basically, everyone I know and don't know. You see, we'll be maintaining to the outside world that you and I are man and wife."

He smiled as if what he said had made perfect sense. Which it did not!

"Your family?" I was flabbergasted. "Your parents?"

He nodded. "Yes. And we'll be stopping by their home on our way to what all will know as our new home. The one I'll be leaving you with at the end of the contract if you're a good girl and do as I say at all times."

His term, good girl, was not making me happy. I was beginning to feel like his puppy or something. "Jett, I think this is a thing you should've told me about before I signed the contract."

"It was in there. It said you had to do as I say at all times and be who I tell you to be. So I am telling you to be Mrs. Jett Simmons. There are worse things to lie about."

"Your family will know me. Am I to tell this lie forever?" He hadn't thought things through. "And I'm not a good liar. Words that aren't true kind of gum up in my mouth and my eyes get really big. This will never work. You may as well head back to the club and let's end the contract now before I make a fool out of you."

He put his arm around me, leaned in close and planted his lips on mine. With no kind of warning, he just kissed me, and I melted into him as if we'd kissed many times before that one. Parting my lips, I invited him in. Our tongues gently rolled around together. He tasted better than I thought he would. He made a fire rise inside of me. And I didn't want to go back and end the contract any longer!

His strong hands moved over my shoulders, cradling my back and pulling me in close to him. My breasts smashed against his hard chest. I curled my hands around the lapels of his suit jacket and hung on for dear life.

Could I lie for him?

Could I make words come out of my mouth in a flowing manner that wouldn't give him away?

Our kiss grew and grew until we were pawing at one another with a need for more. He pulled back, both of us panting. "You sure you want to end this?"

All I could do was shake my head and wait for him to kiss me again.

Which he did, thankfully. He pushed me back on the seat, his weight falling on me like a comfy blanket.

I ran my hands under his jacket to feel his muscular back and moaned with how good those big muscles felt. He pushed my legs apart and laid on me, grinding his erection against me.

He had me then. I was hooked. I'd do my best to make people believe we were married. But I had a ton of questions that I couldn't even ask him, per his rule. I could see things might get a bit on the frustrating side with him.

But as he kissed me into submission, I couldn't seem to care about anything except how good he could make me feel. My body had sensations it never had before. Jett was making me high with just his kiss. What would happen to me when he actually took me?

He eased the passionate kiss and looked at me as he brushed my hair back. "You're exquisite, my little Asia. I knew I had to have you the moment I laid eyes on your picture. I'm impressed by you. I want to warn you, though. I'm a strict man. I don't like small talk or dilly dallying around things. I'm a straightforward man, and I want you to be that way with me too. If you don't like something I do to you, tell me. Honesty is always the number one rule."

"I understand." I was getting lost in his sea green eyes. I ran my hand over his smooth cheek. "May I say that I think you're also exquisite?"

His lips quirked to one side then he nuzzled my neck. "I'm glad you think so."

I pushed my hands through his thick hair, releasing an earthy scent. Breathing it in, I found my head going light again. I had no idea a complete stranger could arouse me so much. Maybe something was really wrong with me. Maybe I'd held onto my virginity too long. It wasn't normal what I was doing, falling into Jett, a man I didn't know.

"Is this what normally happens when you get a new sub?"

His lips grazed their way up my neck as he moved his head up to look at me. "No."

"Do you think something's wrong with me that I'm so aroused by you?" I had to know and had no one else around to ask.

"No."

"Okay..." I didn't know what else to say. He obviously didn't want to talk. He really was a man of few words, it seemed.

"I've picked the right woman to play the part of my wife, that's all it is. We have tons of natural chemistry. Our bodies have accepted that. It might take a while for our minds to catch up, but it's there, and it's stronger than any I've had with anyone else. How about you?"

"Me? I've never had chemistry with anyone before. You're the first."

His lips touched mine briefly, but it still sent heat straight to my core. Then he looked into my eyes with a sultry gaze. "I will be your first, Asia, in many ways."

I gulped, involuntarily. "Yes, you will."

# 11

# JETT

I couldn't keep my hands off her. She was like a drug to me. One I couldn't get enough of. We moved from the car to the jet I'd chartered and were heading to New York. The first stop was at my parents' home in Manhattan. That's where we'd be grilled about our relationship.

Toying with Asia's hand as we sat, side by side, in the beige leather seats, I found it was a perfect time to tell her about our whirlwind romance and marriage. "My mother's name is Jenny, and my father's name is Frank."

"Okay." She gave me a smile. "I can remember that."

"You and I met at a nightclub in Los Angeles."

"I was on vacation out there, wasn't I?" She grinned. "We may as well keep my part in your little fairy tale real. You know, the truth about where I come from and go to college. I'm sure to mess up if everything's a lie."

"You're right. You get to stay you, entirely. I like your whole tale anyway. So you were on vacation with your college roommate." I paused to see if she'd fill in the blank.

"Stacy and I were at the club?"

I filled in that one. “Banshee. I saw you from across the crowded room and went straight to you, asking you to dance.”

“That’s when you found out I’m a lousy dancer.”

I frowned. I couldn’t see her as being a lousy dancer at all. “Which I quickly taught you, and you became fantastic in no time. After we had danced the night away, we ditched Stacy and went to eat at a nearby diner named Lola’s Eatery.”

“I ordered waffles.”

“I ate scrambled eggs and toast.”

She kissed my cheek. “I let you drive me to my hotel.”

“Motel 6.”

She nodded. “You walked me to the door, and I let you kiss me on the cheek, nothing more than that. I’m a good girl.”

I found her utterly adorable and tweaked her little nose. “That you are. I got your number and called you on my way home. We talked until dawn.”

“Then you asked me out for dinner the next night, and the night after that, and the next one too. We became inseparable while I was in L.A. then I had to go back to New Brunswick to school.”

“Ah, yes, back to school you went, and we missed each other so much we couldn’t stand it. That’s when we knew it was true love that we shared.” I kissed her sweet lips. “I asked you to marry me when I flew in to surprise you last week.”

A blush covered her cheeks. “And I accepted and cried when you did.”

Ending our little story, I said, “I scooped you up, took you to Vegas where we made it legal. I’d bought us a home in Harrison, New York before I even proposed, certain you’d say yes.”

“I think I can remember all of that.” She grinned. “I’ll let you do the talking, though. I don’t want to mess it up.”

“There’s one more thing we should practice.” I leaned in close and kissed the soft spot behind her right ear. “Saying, I love you.” Moving back, I looked at her. “And sounding like we mean it. You go first.”

She looked as if she was trying not to laugh. “Jett, I love you.” Her lips then squished into a flat line as she tried not to smile.

"Asia, I love you." I kissed her cheek. "Again."

She ran her hand over my cheek then through my hair as she gazed into my eyes. "I love you," her words were soft, sweet, and sounded so real my heart skipped a beat.

"Do you really?" I didn't even know I was going to ask that question.

She nodded then leaned in and kissed my lips. "I love you, Jett Simmons."

I heated up so quickly it surprised me. My cock thumped as it began to swell. "I love you, Asia Simmons." The words were rolling off my tongue with ease as my desire for her grew.

Running my hands up and down her arms, I was about to take her to the bedroom. But the steward came out with our lunch, spoiling that. "Lobster and steak. I'll bring the white wine right out." He placed the meals on the table.

Taking her by the hand, I helped her up, and we went to eat, instead of going to do what I really wanted to, make out in the privacy of the bedroom. "Come, wife. Have some lunch with your husband."

She giggled, and I liked the way it sounded. Holding the chair out for her, she took the seat I'd offered, and I took the one across from her.

"This looks delicious, Jett."

"I'm glad you like it. So tell me about your family. I should know a little about them."

"My mother's name is Patty and Dad's is Bryan. I have two older sisters."

I cut a piece of steak and found it was cooked exactly the way I liked it. Seemed it was my lucky day. "So you're the baby of the family then?"

"I am." She took a bite of lobster after dipping it into butter and nodded as she chewed and swallowed. "This is great."

"I agree. So what are your sister's names?" I dug into the lobster to try a bite of it.

"Rainbow, or Bow as we call her for short, is married to Stewart. He's a forest ranger. They just took their three kids, Jana, Hailey, and Baxter, and moved to Alaska. Then there's Spring and Max, they live in South Dakota, and they have a baby that's due next month. It's a surprise what they're having."

"Next month? Won't you want to go see your new niece or nephew?" I paused my eating to see if that was a thing she might want to do.

"I'd like to, but I've done this now. I'll go after the summer is over." She cut into her steak and looked it over.

"Is it done to your taste?"

She smiled. "I love it rare. It's as if you already knew me when you ordered this meal, Jett."

"To be honest, I ordered what I like, the same way I've done with all my subs. It's just a coincidence that you like your steak the same way." I smiled though. It was nice that we were on the same wavelength

"Lucky me." She looked a bit disturbed by what I'd said. I didn't like that look on her face.

"I'm sorry. I can be self-absorbed and crass. I'll try to curtail that as much as I can. So, what other things do you like? So that I know when people ask." I gave the steward a frown as he finally came back with the wine. He filled our glasses then left us without saying a word of apology. The guy was earning a spot on my shit-list.

"My favorite meal is boring, spaghetti."

"What's boring about that? I love it too. Especially when it's served with..."

She laughed as she broke in to add, "Homemade meatballs!"

"And don't forget the garlic bread."

We laughed, and I thought things were going so well. Too well. It couldn't be this way for long. Then it occurred to me that she might be acting.

"And for dessert?" she asked then popped a bit of meat into her little mouth.

I went out on a limb and said something I didn't like to see how she'd react. "Lemon pie."

"No," she said as she shook her head. "Apple pie."

"A la Mode?" I asked with surprise.

"Is there any other way?"

She'd hit on my favorite desert. We were well-matched. She wasn't acting at all. And that scared me. Asia Jones was perfect for me. Not just as my sub or fake wife. As a real life partner. And I wasn't ready for that at all!

As we finished lunch, I sat there, secretly hoping there was something about her I'd find unattractive or unlikable. Something that would make it easier to let her go when the three months was up.

The steward came back to pick up our empty plates, and Asia looked at him, asking with a smile, "You don't happen to have any coconut rum and sprite back there, do you? I'm not a huge fan of wine."

He looked down his nose at her, instantly pissing me off. "We only have the finest wines on board. Nothing of poor taste is served on this plane."

And that was it. I got up, towering over the little son of a bitch. "A simple, no ma'am would've sufficed, you little sawed off…"

Asia's hand on my arm stopped me. "It's okay, Jett."

I turned to look at her. "You won't be disrespected in front of me, Asia." I looked back at the man who was foolish enough to talk that way to the woman I was with. "Apologize now."

His face went pale, and his Adam's apple bobbed in his scrawny throat. "I'm sorry, ma'am."

"It's okay." Asia went back to take a seat by the window. Her face had fallen a bit. And that made me want to ring the little shit of a man's throat.

"I'm going to report you, you know." I turned and went to sit down next to her as the man took our things and scurried away. I took Asia's hand and kissed it. "I'm sorry about that."

She cut her eyes at me. "Really, you don't have to be. I was stupid for asking for something so low class in the first place."

"What's low class about some sprite and rum? They serve that at all the expensive beach resorts. That guy's just an ass. Our home will be filled with anything and everything you want, Asia. And I'll let you go see your sister's baby when the time comes."

"You will?" She looked surprised. "You mean it?"

I nodded. "It's a special time in your life. Of course, I mean it."

"Thank you. That means a lot to me." She closed her eyes and laid her head down on my shoulder. “You’re very nice, Jett. That meal made me sleepy.”

“Perhaps a nap in the bedroom is in order.” I got up and took her hand, leading her to the bedroom, aware her eyes were as big as saucers.

Was she afraid to be alone in a bedroom with me?

## 12

# ASIA

I followed behind Jett as he led me to the bedroom. It wasn't my lifelong dream to lose my virginity in the bedroom of a private jet. Although that might sound cool to others, I wanted a traditional memory of that time.

The bed was covered with a deep blue silky bedspread. Plump pillows were at the head of it; they looked inviting. Jett sat me on the side of the bed and pulled one foot up, taking off my shoe. Then he did the same to the other. "There, that'll make you more comfortable." He stepped out of his shoes and took off his jacket, hanging it in the closet. "Lie back, relax."

I did as he said, wondering if he was going to undress me. He unbuttoned the white shirt he wore underneath the jacket and took it off too. I closed my eyes. His body was too perfect; it was making my mouth water.

His body touched mine as he laid down beside me. I was tense as hell, as I waited for his next move. He inched his hand to take mine. "Have a nice nap, Mrs. Simmons."

It seemed that's all we were going to do. Nap.

I was surprised and kind of disappointed too. When I heard his breathing get even and deep, I knew he was out. I opened my eyes and turned over, resting my palm on his chiseled abs.

I'd never felt anything like that before. They were hard as rocks, and they looked like little hills that were split by defined lines. I moved my hand up to run over his mountainous pecs.

His skin was tan and hair-free. I didn't know if he was waxed or if he was naturally hair-free on his chest. All I knew was I found it very appealing. My eyes moved down his body until I found the bulge in his pants.

With a feather-light touch, I moved my hand down and rested it on that bulge, trying to figure out just how big it was. It was longer than my hand, and that was in a non-erect condition. My Lord, how long would it be when he was aroused?

Easing my hand to move around it, I found it thick. My inner thighs pulsed as I went wet. That would be inside me sometime in the near future, and my body was happy about that.

My eyes were growing heavy, and I was slipping into sleep.

I woke to something throbbing against my palm. I'd fallen asleep with my hand on Jett's dick!

And he was moving around, turning toward me, throwing his arm over me then moving closer. He pressed his growing cock against me and moaned. Yet he was still asleep.

I was worried he'd make a move on me as I'd made one on him, while we were sleeping!

I tried to move back, but he threw his leg over me, stopping me in my tracks. I was stuck, and then his hands began to run all over me. Up and down my arm then around to my back and he pulled me closer to him. "Asia," he moaned.

"Jett, are you awake?" I tapped his shoulder.

"Um, hm..." He inched forward and kissed me.

It wasn't right what his kisses did to me. They went straight to my head and rendered me mindless. My hands moved on their own to run over his naked back. His skin felt warm and inviting as I caressed it. Our mouths melded into one as our bodies moved to get even closer.

I was completely lost in him. Every move he made, every touch, was felt intensely. His hand ran up my leg, pushing my dress up. His hand rested on my hip, holding me as he pressed that big cock against my pulsing pantie covered pussy.

Rolling over me, he pinned me to the bed then his mouth left mine as he trailed kisses down my throat and over my dress covered breasts. He made his way all the way down until his hot mouth was on my panties.

The look he gave me when he looked up at me made my heart fly at light speed. He took the top of my panties in his teeth and moved them down only enough to expose part of me.

He kissed my pearl, and I moaned with desire. He smiled then kissed it again and again until I began to writhe with pleasure. Moving his hands to cup my ass, he lifted me off the bed and licked me over and over.

His dark waves were brushing against my stomach; he had my dress pushed up so far. I ran my hands through them as I watched him kissing me in a place I'd never been kissed before.

It was far better than what I thought it would feel like. I was completely wet, and the moaning I was doing just couldn't be stopped. Just when I thought I was about to explode, he kissed my inner thigh. I was panting like a dog, then mewling like a cat. What he was doing to me wasn't humanly possible, I thought.

If that was what sex felt like, how did people ever stop doing it?

It was fantastic!

He bit the inside of my leg, and an insane amount of adrenaline shot through me. Jett got up, looking down at me with lust-filled eyes. "I'm about to ruin you for other men, Asia." He ripped my panties off with one hard yank. I whimpered with a small amount of fear and a large amount of need.

Jett took me by the waist and lifted me all the way up, putting my legs over his broad shoulders. My pussy was in his face as he licked me up and down, running his tongue through every part of me. Then it was inside me, and I grabbed handfuls of his hair as it felt amazing. He moved me up and down as his tongue slid in and out of me.

I had no idea how he was lifting me so much. It was as if I didn't weigh a thing. I was close to climaxing, and my body was shivering. He moved his tongue out of me and sucked on my clit. It sent me over the edge, and I shrieked with the hard orgasm.

Then he was back inside me, licking up all I had released for him. I was shaking with how intense it all was. He was right; he had ruined me for other men. Who else could handle me the way he had? Who else could make me feel the way he did?

No one could. I knew that even then. I was his. I belonged to Jett Simmons. But only for a few months and I knew I'd want to belong to him a hell of a lot longer than that.

How did I get so caught up in him so damn quickly?

He laid me back on the bed and wiped his mouth with the back of his hand as he breathed raggedly and looked at me like a lion looks at a gazelle. "You taste better than anything I've ever had in my mouth, Asia."

Heat filled my cheeks. "Thank you." I had no idea what one should say to a remark like that.

He pulled a piece of luggage out of the closet and put it on the bed, opened it and took out a pair of lacy white panties. He eased them up my legs, covering me back up.

I wanted to ask why we weren't going to do more, pop that pesky cherry of mine, but just before my mouth opened, the pilot told us to take our seats, we were about to land in New York.

I sighed, heavily and saw a smile curve his lips. "Disappointed?"

With a nod, I rolled out of bed. "I guess I should check my hair and makeup before we depart."

What I saw when I looked in the little bathroom mirror shocked me. My hair was a mess! My makeup was gone!

I closed the door and went to the bathroom, finding that it stung when I peed. "Ow!"

I could hear his deep chuckle. "Sorry about that. It's a nasty side-effect."

My cheeks heated as I realized he'd heard me. All finished, I got up, washed my hands and used some more water to calm my hair back into place. I splashed some water on my face and at least looked refreshed, instead of freshly fucked.

But I hadn't been fucked. He'd left me a virgin. I supposed he had another time in mind to take my virginity. But he could toy with me like that for as long he wanted to. I didn't mind one bit!

# 13

# JETT

With my hand on her knee, Asia and I sat on my parents' leather sofa as they stared at us. "So you really did it?" my father asked.

I held up Asia's left hand, showing off the rings. "We did. Last night. In Vegas."

The lies were kind of choking me. It wasn't as easy to lie right to their faces. It was much easier to do over the phone.

"And you're from L.A.?" Mom asked Asia.

"No, ma'am, I was raised in Queens. I go to college at Rutgers in Jersey. I was on vacation when I met Jett."

I was glad she remembered our little story because I was the one who was finding myself stumbling over the lies. "At a night club," I managed to add.

"The Banshee," Asia said as she patted my hand that was resting on her knee. "He taught me how to dance. Up until I met him, I thought I had two left feet. He was a fantastic teacher."

"You made it easy." I kissed her cheek. Out of the corner of my eye, I saw my mother smile. "Then we went to eat after ditching her friend, Stacy."

"Lola's Eatery, Jett had scrambled eggs and toast."

"Asia had waffles." I was enamored with her. "And then I took her to the Motel 6 where she and Stacy were staying. I left her on the doorstep with one kiss to her perfectly pink cheek."

Asia gazed into my eyes, and I felt as if the lies had really happened. I could see it all in my head as if it had been real. Her rosebud lips parted. "I knew I loved him even then."

"You did?" I found myself asking.

She nodded. "From that little kiss and that wonderful night, I knew you were the one."

"I had a strong idea you were the one for me too." I looked at my parents who had their mouths hanging open as they looked at me with disbelieving expressions. "Anyway, we went out every night she was in town, and when she went back to school, the miles between us only made it sink in more. We'd found love. So I went to surprise her the day before yesterday."

"He came to my dorm room. He got down on one knee and asked me to make him the happiest man in the world. I cried as I quickly accepted his proposal." Asia ran the back of her hand over my cheek. "I'm so happy you asked."

"I'm so happy you accepted."

"So you went to Vegas and got married," Mom said, taking our attention. "And now what will you do?"

"I bought us a house in the Sterling Ridge area of Harrison, New York. I thought it'd be a perfect place to live and raise a family." I ran my hand over Asia's cheek. "We can't wait to get started."

My father cleared his throat. "What about your job in L.A.?"

How could I have forgotten about that piece of the puzzle?

Panic had to have shown on my face as Asia's eyes went wide and then she smiled. "Oh, he can still take care of things in L.A. he has a wonderful assistant he's been training to take over for him when he's here. Isn't that right, honey?"

"Yeah, Seth Rogers is the man who's watching over things while I take the next three months off. I'll go to Los Angeles Monday through Thursday and spend the other three nights at home with Asia. I've figured it all out."

"Okay, sounds like you've thought things through then." Dad

looked relieved. "One day I'll want you back here anyway. You'll take over the CEO position, and you'll have to be here. Maybe this Rogers guy will be suitable to take over your place in L.A. altogether."

"I can groom him for it."

Mom got up and gestured for us to follow her. "Dinner is being served in the formal dining room. Hilda should have the appetizer on the table already. Come on."

Taking Asia's hand, I helped her up, and we followed a bit behind my parents. "You're better at lying than you said you were."

"It's important to me to help you, Jett. I guess I see it as my job."

The idea that she was looking at this as a job didn't sit right with me. I wanted her to like it. "Are you having a nice time?"

She nodded. "I am."

"I can't wait to see the house with you. I bought it without ever going to see it. I've only seen pictures online. It's completely furnished, and I had a stylist fill the closet and dresser with clothes and shoes for you."

Asia lit up like a Christmas tree. "Oh my God! Really!"

My parents stopped and turned to look at us. Mom's left brow was cocked. "What's so exciting?"

"I just gave Asia another surprise. She hasn't seen the house yet. I told her I had a stylist fill the closet for her." I wrapped my arm around Asia. "She's got a whole new wardrobe."

"That's sweet of you, Jett." Mom turned around and kept walking. "You're just so different."

Asia leaned on me and put her hand on my chest. "That's nice to hear. I like that."

"What, that I'm different?"

"Yes. It means I bring something out in you no one ever has."

And she was right about that. Asia did bring things out in me no one ever had. While I was on a high from it, I knew there'd come a time when I'd hate it. I'd want to be the old me. The hard as nails man who no one could hurt.

I hadn't avoided love, but I certainly hadn't sought it out. I purchased subs to fill the void I'd feel at times. Other than that, I didn't like to date anyone more than a few times.

Asia would be the one woman I'd spend more time with than I had with anyone. She and I were getting along better than I'd anticipated. But it would have to come to an end, like all things.

We sat at the table, me right next to Asia. I held her hand on top of the table and saw my mother looking at our hands. "You said something about getting started on a family soon. I hope you two think long and hard about that. You've rushed into this marriage. There's no reason to rush into having kids. They really change your life. Why not take a year to get to know one another before you start trying to add kids into things?"

"Maybe Mom's right, Asia."

"Anything you want, I want, Jett. You know that. I love you." The words popped out of her mouth so naturally, it was like she really meant them.

"I love you too. We'll talk about it more later on." I turned my attention to Mom. "Thanks for the advice. We're just so in love; we might not be thinking straight right now."

"I can see that," Mom said as she looked from me to Asia. "You both are glowing."

Were we?

I had no idea.

Was I actually falling in love?

I couldn't let that happen. I wasn't out to hurt Asia. I also wasn't out to fall in love with her, either.

I crossed my fingers that something would crop up soon that I couldn't stand about her. It happened all the time with other women. One snored, one had ugly feet, one had an annoying laugh. I'm sure something Asia did would bother me, eventually.

Love wasn't on the cards for me. I didn't want it.

Love made you weak. It made you vulnerable. I wanted no part of it.

"The family vacation is in a couple of weeks. Did you tell Asia about it, Jett?" Mom asked as the maid brought in a tray of smoked meats and cheeses along with a bottle of red wine.

"I did, Mom. Hello, Daisy, is there any coconut rum and a lemon lime cola in the house?" I asked her as I remembered that Asia wasn't fond of wine.

"Yes, sir. Should I mix you up a drink?"

"Mix one for my wife, Asia."

Daisy's hand went to her heart as she gasped. "Your wife, sir?"

"Asia, this is Daisy, the kitchen maid. Daisy, this is my wife."

Daisy came and shook Asia's hand. "Oh my goodness, you're so lovely. How lucky for Mr. Jett to find a woman like you."

"Thank you." A blush covered Asia's cheeks. "I think I'm the lucky one."

"I'll get you that drink, ma'am. It's nice to meet you." Daisy ran off to make the drink, leaving Asia looking at me with a curious expression.

"She seemed quite surprised. You're only twenty-eight, not quite a spinster." Asia laughed.

"See, Mom. I'm not so old."

"His lifestyle is what had everyone worried about him never marrying." Mom picked up some meat and cheese. "He's never even had a steady girlfriend. That's why you'll see a lot of the family will be shocked by this marriage. No one saw it coming. Not with how Jett is."

"Was," I corrected her. "I was that way. Asia changed that."

"Let's hope so." Mom took a drink.

Dad shook his head. "Let's not jinx them, darling. People can change."

I was beginning to wonder if he was right. Could I change? Could I become a man who only wanted one woman and wanted her around most of the time?

I didn't think I could be that man. Yet, I had tied myself down to one woman for a matter of three months, just to avoid being setup by my friends and family. Why would I do such a thing?

It was out of character for me. I was that guy who'd tell everyone to fuck off and leave me the hell alone. Instead of doing that, I'd intentionally set myself up with a woman I'd have to be with for the longest period of time I'd been with anyone.

Had I subconsciously created a situation I intentionally avoided at all costs, to prove something to myself? Was Asia in the right place at the right time? Or was it bigger than that?

Things were falling into place a little too well. Was serendipity stepping in to take over my life?

## 14

# ASIA

The day had been long, I rested my head on Jett's shoulder as his parents' driver took us to Harrison to our new home. One mansion after the next we passed until we turned into a gated entrance. "This is it, Asia. This will be all yours after this is over." He kissed the side of my head, sweetly.

I should've been over the moon. Instead, I felt a sharp pain in my gut with what he'd said, when this is over. I didn't want to think in those terms. I genuinely liked the man. Thinking about when it all would end wasn't a thing I wanted to think about.

The gates opened after the driver put in the code Jett called out to him and in we went, winding down the long drive. "The lot is two acres, the house is just over twelve-thousand square feet. There's a pool in the back and a six car garage. I know that's pretty small as far as garages go."

"Small?" I was in awe as we pulled up to the front of the house. House? No, it was much more than a mere house. It was a palace! Stone statues of robust women, reminding me of old Roman statues, were on both sides of the wide staircase that led up to the green front door. There was a fountain in the area in the middle of the driveway that became a circle. A bevy of mermaids flowed up the middle and looked as if they were playfully splashing one another.

The white of the bricks that served as the siding was so pristine the place seemed to glow. It had two storeys, and a balcony came off one of the rooms upstairs. It made a nice shaded area over the front entrance. Gray, green English ivy covered the exterior, making it look like it had been there forever. “Jett, this is beyond anything I could’ve imagined.”

“Does that mean you like it?” He chuckled as he got out of the car and took my hand to help me out.

The evening breeze was cool and gentle. The smells were wonderful, earthy tones, mixed with sweet flowers, and somewhere in the rich neighborhood, someone was grilling outdoors. “Jett, I have no idea how I’ll ever explain this place to my family.”

“I’ll help you come up with something. Hell, you can tell them the same thing we’re telling everyone else.” He led me up the stairs and tapped in a code on the door. “565679, is the code to all the doors and the gate. There’s a security system that automatically locks the doors and gate once they close. You’ll be safe at all times.”

The foyer was large, and the ceiling was high, the tones from outside carried on to the inside. No furniture was in the room, but there were more Romanesque statues and gorgeously green, potted plants. “It’s just so, so…” I didn’t have the words to describe it.

“So far, everything is pleasing you then?” Jett gave me a million dollar smile, and I couldn’t hold back any longer.

Throwing my arms around him, I kissed his cheek. “Everything is more than pleasing. You’re the kindest, most generous man in the entire world!”

His strong arms held me as his warm breath stirred the hair by my ear. “You’re the sweetest woman I’ve ever met, Asia. I mean that.”

We toured the house, finding one living area after another before we came to an enormous kitchen. “OMG! Jett, this is remarkable!” Shiny stainless steel covered the stove that was like a mile long. “Where’s the fridge?”

Jett smiled as he pulled open what I thought were walls and there were not one, but three refrigerators. "And across the room over there are the freezers." He pointed to a glass door that was underneath the long island bar. "That's a wine chiller. Since you don't care for wine, you can fill it with any other beverage of your choice."

"Jett, this is all too much. I can't take this. I can't!" Tears welled up in my eyes as I was overcome with emotion.

He wrapped his arms around me, hugging me tightly. "You can take this. I want you to have it all, Asia. It's a big deal, what you're doing for me."

I shook my head as I continued to cry. "It's not that big of a deal. I don't deserve all this."

"You do. You're giving up a huge part of yourself to me. I'm not taking that lightly."

"If you're talking about my virginity, it's not worth all that you're paying me." I sniffled, and he moved back with me until he could reach a napkin.

Handing it to me, he said, "Blow your nose. Dry those pretty eyes and stop thinking about the money and things. I have it to give to you, let me do that for all you're doing for me."

Nodding, I didn't want to make him upset with me. I decided I'd deal with my emotions on my own. It wasn't for him to have to deal with anyway. "I'm sorry, Jett."

"Don't be. I should've known you'd be overwhelmed. You'll get used to it all in no time. There are a few things you should know. A maid comes in three times a week, Mondays, Wednesdays, and Fridays. She was the previous owner's maid and had worked here for years. I kept her on. There's a gardener who comes once a week. A maintenance man also comes once a week, he takes care of the pool and anything that needs fixing. I'll be purchasing a town car and hiring a driver for it, as well."

I tried to suck up the emotions that were bubbling up inside of me. "Okay. I'll pay their wages once I get the money from escrow."

"No, I've taken care of all that. Their salaries are already set up to be automatically deducted from one of my bank accounts. I'll pay them for you."

"You'll pay the people who'll take care of what will be my house, forever?" I shook my head. "One day you'll get married, and your wife won't like that."

"I'm in charge of my money and what I pay. No woman's going to tell me a thing about that." He walked around to get a couple of bottles of water out of the fridge closest to him. "Now let's go see the rest of the house. There are ten bedrooms, all have en-suites with private lavatories and walk in closets."

His arrogant attitude about women was an eye-opener and the first time I'd seen that side of him. I couldn't say I liked it. But he wasn't my man to correct. I was his woman, not the other way around.

There was one bedroom downstairs that we found. I thought it was the master, but he informed me it was only a guest bedroom. The rest of them were up a grand staircase made out of Mahogany. The railing and steps shone like something out of a museum.

It wasn't melding into my brain the place would be mine. It was just too good to be true!

"This will be our room." He opened the first door on the left, and I went dumb.

A bed, larger than any one I'd ever seen, sat in the middle of the enormous room. Dark wood, ornate carvings and a beige veil that hung across the top of the canopy took my breath away. An emerald jacquard comforter was spread out over it. It was the most opulent piece of bedroom furniture I'd ever seen. An entire dark brown leather living room set was in one corner, and there was a giant television hanging on the wall in that area.

"Jett, this is stunning!"

He took my hand, leading me to a door on the right. When he opened it, a light came on, and I found we were standing inside a closet with only women's clothing in it. "Your things are in here."

"God! Oh, dear God!" I had to put my hand over my mouth to cover how it was gaping. I turned and hugged him. "Jett, you're too much!"

"The door next to this one is full of my things. I'll have them moved when this is over."

There it was again, the sharp pain in my gut whenever he talked about it being over. I looked at him as I shook my head. "You'll always have a home here, Jett. Always."

Now it was his turn to get glassy-eyed. "You mean that?"

With a nod, I took his hand and held it to my heart. "I want you to always think of this place as your home too." I meant it. I could never see myself being there with any other man.

He chuckled as he took me across the room. "Let me show you the bathroom. And don't go handing out invitations just yet, Asia. One day you will marry, and your husband may not want your old Dom hanging around."

The thought sent a shiver down my spine. And as he opened the door to what looked like a spa, I gasped. "Jett!"

A shower with more jets than I knew what to do with was in one corner. A giant Jacuzzi tub filled the opposite corner. "I can see some fun times in here. Can you?" Jett gave me a squeeze and picked me up, taking me back to the bedroom. "And now to try out this bed. What do you say, are you ready to get your mind blown some more? I've got all night to make you mine."

Was I ready for what he was about to do?

# 15

# JETT

Pushing open the French doors that led to the balcony, I let in a cool breeze as night took over. The day had been long, the night would feel even longer.

I was about to take Asia!

I'd dreamt of being intimate with her since the day I saw her pretty face on my computer screen. The time had come, and I was allowing her some time to bathe and get herself ready for me.

The entire house had been stocked, the bathrooms had scented soaps and expensive hair care products. I wanted Asia to see how the other half, a half she was now a part of, lived.

Standing on the balcony, I looked around, seeing only tall trees that shielded the home away from prying eyes. Asia would be safe in a place like this. I'd ensured her safety and wealth for what she was doing for me and giving me.

Crickets chirped, and the other insects joined in for a nightly chorus. I left the balcony to go across the hall and take a quick shower to make myself presentable too.

Hot water washed over my body that was tense with anticipation. I'd never had a virgin before. I'd never been a gentle lover. Admittedly, I was a selfish lover. But I didn't want to be that way with Asia. The young woman deserved more.

I had thought of her often since that first day. There had never been a woman who I'd thought about as much as I did her. And I made tons of mental plans for her as well. The house, everything in it, her clothes and what she'd look best in were all on my mind. But mostly I thought about how I'd make her first time special and memorable. It was almost like a script that ran through my head of what we'd do. I wanted to touch every last inch of her as she lay on the bed, quivering with desire. I wanted to slowly bring her to a state of arousal then keep her there for hours on end. We could sleep the day away tomorrow. Tonight was for making memories that would last her a lifetime.

I thought those memories might be pretty special to me too.

With nothing more than a towel wrapped around my waist, I padded back across the hallway to our bedroom. And that's where I found my little Asia, waiting in bed for me. The blanket pulled up to her chin as she peeked at me. "I'm ready, sir."

Shaking my head, I made my way to her. "No, don't call me that. This is about you, Asia. It's all about you. I don't want you to think I paid for this and you have to give me what I want."

Her brow furrowed. "So you don't want me?"

"I do want you." I took a seat next to her and pulled the blanket down to expose her breasts. They were delectable. It was hard to pull my eyes away from them as my mouth watered to taste them. "Do you want me?"

She breathed deeply. "More than I knew I would." She took my hand and placed it on her breast. "Yours is the first hand to touch this."

I felt her heart beating fast beneath my hand. "Asia, you have no idea how much I hunger for you."

"I have a bit of an idea because I have that hunger as well. Jett, you will be gentle, won't you?" Her eyes held a little fear, and it pulled at my heart.

"I will be very gentle with you, my little Asia." I leaned in to kiss her sweet lips and found them quivering.

I wanted to calm her, ease those fears that later would seem irrational. I was only going to bring her pleasure, there was nothing to fear. As a virgin, she didn't know that.

Assuming she knew there'd be a little pain when I first entered her, I didn't know if I should bring that up or not. I decided not to talk about anything. Instead, I unwrapped the towel that was covering me and took her hand, placing it on my not yet fully erect cock.

Our eyes were glued to the others, then she broke our stare and looked at the thing that would soon end her innocence. She ran her hand up and down it. "It's soft. Like silk that's covering a hard cylinder. I've never felt anything like it." Her eyes went to mine. "May I put my mouth on it?"

I sighed and wanted nothing more than to feel her soft lips moving up and down my girth. But the night wasn't about me, she could explore me another night. The night was all about her. I shook my head. "You lie back and let me show you what the big deal is with sex."

She snuggled into the pillow. "Take me, Jett. I am yours."

"And for tonight, I am yours too, Asia. Tonight we make love. For the first time in your life and mine."

Lines formed between her brows as confusion filled her beautiful face. "For the first time for you? I don't understand."

"I've had sex. I've never made love to a woman. Tonight will be a first for us both."

The smile that curled her rosebud lips made me smile too. "I'm glad to be your first experience then. Shall we dance, my love?"

Like a moth to a flame, I went to her, knowing I was flying too close to the fire. I might get burned if I wasn't careful. I had to be careful!

Our lips met, igniting the fire that would burn throughout the night. Our hands moved over the other's body in slow waves. Then I ended the kiss and pulled away from her. "I want to kiss every inch of you."

She nodded and smiled. "Please proceed."

Pulling the blanket all the way off her, I stood and looked at her perfect little body. Creamy thighs bulged in luscious curves. I ran one fingertip down her leg as I walked to the end of the bed and climbed on.

Her toenails were painted pink, and I kissed each one of the cute little things. The tops of her feet were soft against my lips. Her legs, though short, seemed long as I kissed up one then down the other. I rolled her over and placed my lips on her round and taut ass. She shivered as I did and moaned. I couldn't help but slip a finger into her to check her level of desire, finding her nice and wet.

She'd become a whole lot wetter before I would claim her!

I kissed her back, shoulders and neck as I straddled her body, letting my cock graze over her warm flesh. I pressed it against her ass, humping her a bit, but not penetrating her at all.

I could feel her body growing hotter. And mine wasn't far behind. My entire body was tingling in a way I'd never experienced. I was letting it all go. My mind was as into it as much as my body was, for once.

Kissing my way down her back, I focused on her ass, kissing it and flicking my tongue around her rectum. As I eased it in, she moaned, "God that feels good, Jett."

Kissing her while stroking her asshole with my tongue, I began to take her to the point of orgasm. Asia would be sore from head to toe by morning. That was okay, we had a magnificent Jacuzzi tub to pummel her aching body, and she'd soon be ready to go some more. I'd make her crave my touch before I was through. The way I was craving her.

Finally, I'd satisfy my craving!

## 16

## ASIA

Getting my ass kissed was pretty damn great. Who knew?

Jett's fingers gripped the front of my hips, lifting me so he could push his tongue deeper into a place I didn't know I'd like such a thing. He moved one hand around me until he found my clit and pushed it as if it was an on-off button. Over and over he did that as his tongue moved in and out of my ass.

A wave washed over me as I began to climax. I moaned and purred as it moved all the way through me, from the top of my head, clean to my toes. "Jett, oh, Jett, yes…" I trailed off as he stopped what he was doing to turn me over and push his tongue inside of me.

He made a deep, guttural groan as he tongue-fucked me. His thick, wavy hair was damp against my skin. I couldn't help but tangle my hands in it. I hoped he'd never cut that gorgeous head of hair he had going on.

When he'd had his fill of me there, he moved up my body, trailing hot kisses over my stomach then taking one of my breasts in his mouth as he looked at me. I watched him run his tongue around the nipple then pulled on it with his lips. It hurt a bit but sent a strange sensation deep into the pit of my stomach.

I had the feeling if he sucked on it long enough, it'd send me into an orgasm. Jett certainly knew his way around a woman's body, I had to give him that!

While he tantalized one tit, he massaged the other then moved his mouth up to nip and suck my neck, a place just behind my ear that made me go wild for him.

With an insane amount of desire, I arched my body up to his, silently begging him to enter me. I wanted him so bad it made my body ache. As if he understood that, he ground his hard cock against me as he bit me mercilessly then stabbed the steely beast into me with one hard push.

The groan I made was from some place deep inside me. It burned, but in a way, I couldn't imagine. A pleasurable burn? Who'd heard of such a thing?

"Oh, Jett! Oh, yeah!"

His expression was one of concern as he raised his head to look at me. "You like it, baby? You doing okay?"

Grasping his gorgeous face between my palms, I smiled as I moved my body up, making his cock go deeper into me. "Oh, yes... I love it. It feels incredible!"

Relief took over his expression, and he kissed me. His tongue was a musky mix of my juices, and I kissed him, hungrily as he made long slow strokes that blew my mind.

Our bodies ebbed and flowed in a way that was mesmerizing to me. I was no longer innocent, I was a woman in every way. I was Jett's woman!

That precious memory would hold a spot in my head, making me his forever. There'd never be another who I'd share that moment with. The moment I was taken by a man. A powerful, handsome man. It felt no less special to me than if I'd waited to do that with a man I loved. At least I felt that way at the time.

Jett was gentle with me, just as he'd promised he'd be. His touch was light, stirring my skin in ways that sent me further into arousal. His tongue fought mine for control, and I gave it to him, willingly.

He moved his hard cock in a rhythm that rocked me like a boat on calm seas. I ran my hands over his hard muscular back, relishing how they rippled with his movements. I ran my foot up the back of his leg and noticed how much deeper it let him go into me.

Easing both legs up, I bent my knees and pulled them up as high as I could. Jett moved one of his arms around one leg and moved it back even further, making his cock thrust deeper into me.

I could barely breathe as my body began to crest. "Jett!"

"Oh, baby, please give it to me. I want it more than I've ever wanted anything. Give me what I need, baby. Give it all to me!" He slammed into me at a furious pace until I was screaming his name over and over as my body climaxed, convulsing tightly around his plunging cock. He made a harsh sound as he jerked inside of me, sending wet heat into me and making my orgasm more intense. "Baby, God!"

"Jett," I moaned as I ran my hands through his hair and he buried his face in my neck.

That was it, the deed had been done. And I felt incredible about it. I worried I might be upset when it finally happened. I thought I might mourn the loss of something I'd held onto so tightly. But in the end, I was elated and had felt things I didn't know it was possible to feel.

"Thank you, Jett. That was a memory I'll treasure forever. And you made me feel spectacular." I pulled his face out of the crook of my neck and kissed him.

He groaned as he kissed me back. Then pulled back and looked at me as he ran his hand over my cheek. "My God, you're one beautiful woman, Asia. I'm not sure I'll ever get enough of you."

I smiled. "Good. Nothing would suit me more than you never ending this." Immediately I knew I'd said the wrong thing by the frown that made creases between his dark brows.

"As good as this is, it won't last forever." He rolled off me and walked to the bathroom as I laid there, perfectly still and wishing I hadn't said what I had.

I didn't mean to ruin the moment for him, and I definitely had. When he came back, I felt the need to apologize, "Jett, I'm sorry." I leaned up on my elbows to look at him so he could see the seriousness in my eyes. “I know this is temporary. It’s just that I loved that and I don’t think anyone else will ever rock my world the way you just did.”

He had a damp wash cloth in his hand and sat on the side of the bed. “Lay back, let me clean you up.” I did as he said to and looked at the ceiling, not particularly loving what he was doing. “I’m sorry I went cold on you, Asia. It’s just that I don’t want you to get hurt.”

He said one thing, but I felt he meant another. I thought he really meant it was him getting hurt that was buried deep in the recesses of his mind. “I understand. That’s very gallant of you, Jett.” I sat up as he was finished with the uncomfortable cleaning. I wanted to tell him I was more than capable of doing that, but the soft look on his face stopped me.

Slowly and softly, he ran his fingertips lightly up the inside of my leg. “Asia, I want you to know that you’re already fast becoming precious to me. I may do things that make you feel like this will go on forever. I don’t want you to take it to heart. I’m not this guy.”

Stroking his cheek, I leaned in and pressed my lips to it. “We can take one day at a time, Jett. No pressure. This is a contract that will be up at the end of August, and we can have fun in the meantime. Like a vacation. I loved it when my family went on a vacation to Miami for a whole week one summer. We all loved it there and wished it would last forever. But when the week ended, we had to go back home to our normal lives. It was bittersweet, but we did it and were left with great memories.”

“Thank you.” He nuzzled my neck. “I’m glad you understand. I love that about you. You’re so understanding.”

“I love that you’re so sweet and generous.”

His lips pressed against my neck. “I love how you opened up for me.”

My body was beginning to heat up again as I ran my hands through his hair. “I love how you took me to a place I’d never been.”

He moved back to look into my eyes. “And I’m about to take you there again, baby. I wanna make you walk funny for a week.”

I laughed as he pushed me back on the bed and climbed over me. I could see our first week together was going to be very enlightening!

# 17

# JETT

Taking a taxi to the Mercedes dealership, I was ready to set us up with cars. One for me, one for her, and one for us both. I had an order in with a chauffeur company, and a car and driver would be showing up for us when we needed it. But I didn't want to arrive everywhere in that style. So a pair of matching Mercedes was what I was shopping for.

Asia was hesitant as we entered the dealership and a salesman came right to us. "Hello, and what is this happy couple looking for today?"

"Asia, what's catching your eye?"

She smiled and looked at the salesman. "What's your cheapest car?"

I chuckled. "No, that's not how we shop for things, baby." I looked at our salesman. "We're Mr. and Mrs. Simmons. And you are?"

He extended his hand to me. "Brett. Nice to meet you both. So, money is no object today?"

"Money's always an object. I just don't want my wife influenced by the price of the car she wants. So leave out the pricing and just give us the details on the cars she likes." I ran my arm around Asia and lead her around the cars on the showroom floor. "And we'll be taking the cars we purchase today off the showroom floor. We don't have time to wait for ordered ones to come in."

"Okay, well as you can see we have plenty available for you to choose from. And did you say cars, plural, more than one?" Brett was seeing commission dollar signs and chomping at the bit to make the sales.

"We're going to get two cars today. Whatever she picks, I'll have the same. But we'll want different colors." I ushered Asia to the car nearest to us.

It was a deep gray color, and she ran her fingers over the smooth surface. "I think this one is pretty."

Brett was quick to point out everything about it, "This is C class C 300 Cabriolet in Selenite gray. With a 4 cylinder engine, that's plenty of power to move the light weight of this car." He opened the door. "Slip inside, Mrs. Simmons."

Asia got in behind the wheel. "Oh, this is nice." She looked up at me. "This leather is so soft and pretty."

"Do you like music, Mrs. Simmons?"

"I do like my jams, Brett." She smiled at him, and I felt a hint of pride at how great she was looking behind the wheel of a nice car and how she was easily interacting with our salesman.

"This little beauty has a Burmester Surround Sound System, and when you add in the fact it comes with satellite radio, well, you have a nightclub on wheels." He laughed and shoved his hands into his pockets.

Asia eyed me. "Jett, what do you think about this car?"

"I think I have never bought a 4 cylinder anything." I looked around to see what else they had.

Quick to spot the increase in price that I wanted, Brett pointed out the S class cars. "Over there we have our 8 cylinder cars."

I helped Asia out of the car and took her to the area where cars that were more my speed were located. I watched her eyes land on a shiny deep blue one. "Oh, Jett, I can see you in that car. Do you like that color?"

"Blue is my favorite color." I pointed at a teal colored one. "I could definitely see you in that. Do you like it?"

"I do. It's so... different. I don't think I've seen that exact color on the road before. These all are a bit on the different color side." She walked up to the one I pointed out, and Brett opened the door for her.

"Oh, wow. How did you make it even more luxurious?"

"Magic," Brett said with a chuckle. "This one has all the bells and whistles Mercedes Benz makes. Lane departure means you'll never run into someone in another lane. Electronic stability means you won't go skidding out of control. There's even a blind spot sensor to watch over you."

"Now this is what I'm talking about. A safe car to put my precious cargo in." I walked around the car and looked it over. "We'll test drive this one, and if we like it, we'll take both the blue one and this one. I expect they have the same features."

"They do, identical except for the colors." Brett was smiling like a madman. I knew we'd chosen the most expensive cars on the lot. With two commissions, he'd be living high on the hog for a while. And he'd most likely get some kind of bonus from his employer for pulling off such a coup.

The test ride was fun for me. I let Asia drive, and she was so nervous it was cute. "Oh, God, Jett! I'm freaking out here!"

"Baby, we haven't even left the parking lot yet."

She nodded and gulped, making me laugh. "It's just a car. Now ease on out there, there's very little traffic."

Pulling out so slowly a turtle could've beaten her, she eased on the gas, and we took off with a smooth start. "Oh, this rides like a dream, Jett." She gave me a sideways glance. "But I know this car must cost a small fortune. We don't have to get two of them. I'll get the 4 cylinder, and you get this one."

"Not a chance in hell, Asia. You get what I do. And this car is safer. I want you to be safe. I want to leave you in a safe home with a safe car." My stomach knotted as I talked about leaving her.

I didn't want to even think about it!

"I know you do, but I'm sure that other car has all those same safety features. We'll ask Brett when we get back. I'm sure that other car will drive just as good as this one does."

"You're going to get this one, Asia. End of discussion."

She frowned, which I thought wasn't even close to the expression she'd should've been wearing. "I don't want you to spend a boatload of money on a car for me."

"And I don't care what you want. I'm buying you this one. We shouldn't be arguing about this. This is a fun time, Asia. Damn!"

She huffed and took a right turn. "I'll be quiet. I don't want you to think I'm ungrateful because I'm super grateful. I just worry about you spending too much money is all."

"I have it to spend. Don't worry about my money. Let me do that. If I tell you to get something, I want you to get the things that are worth what you pay for them. Not some piece of crap that's cheap."

"I wouldn't call that first car a piece of crap, Jett." She made the block, and we were back at the dealership.

"It wasn't as good as this one is. So you just keep those pretty little lips of yours shut so I can make a good deal on the two cars. I'm happy with my purchases. I want you to be happy too."

She parked and looked over the interior once more. "It is the most beautiful car I've ever seen." Our eyes caught. "Thank you. I'll love it forever. I'll take excellent care of it too."

"I'm sure you will. Now let's get inside and do the paperwork. You did bring your ID right?"

"It's in my purse, like always." Brett opened her door, letting her out as I got out of the passenger side.

"And how do we feel about this car, Mrs. Simmons?"

"We feel pretty awesome about it, Brett. I'll leave you to wheel and deal with the hubby about it, though."

I walked up behind her and wrapped my arm around her waist as we headed inside to make a deal. While I wasn't exactly happy with how she'd argued with me, I had to admit that I respected her for doing it. She was no money grabber, that was for sure. And she did have a good head on her shoulders. How was a girl from her poor upbringing supposed to know about things that cost more money than other things of the same nature?

I could teach her about things like that. Asia could learn so much from me. Even though our time would be relatively short, I planned on taking her to another level of life. One she'd probably never even dreamt of.

The vacation with my family was looming in the near future. She'd be hobnobbing with Hamptons' royals. Rubbing elbows with elite New Yorkers. She was about to enter a world she'd become a permanent part of.

It was then that I realized Asia and I would run into one another for the rest of our lives. I was bringing her into my world. A place, even upon a fake divorce, she'd always be a part of.

I hadn't thought that all the way through. Could I see Asia later on in life, perhaps with another man? Could I handle that?

I wasn't sure I could, but I'd already started the train that was bound to derail my entire life.

Might as well enjoy the ride!

# 18

# ASIA

All the way to Jett's parent's vacation home, my stomach was in knots. This was going to be where I'd meet his entire family and the family friends. He'd coached me on what he expected of me. Good manners, which I had already, stay quiet unless asked a direct question, and use the words, I love you, often.

I'd spent two weeks with the man, and those words wouldn't be hard to say at all. I was falling. I mean, it was a head over heels kind of love, and I knew I'd end up crying like a baby when it was all over. But I was trying not to focus on that. I wanted to enjoy each day as it came and, most of the time, left the ending of it all out of my head.

We'd left early that morning, he drove us in his new car. Mine stayed behind in the garage at home. A home that was going to be mine, all alone, in a matter of a few months. I had no idea how I'd feel about being alone in that house or in our bedroom.

With the top down, we drove in the cool morning air, enjoying the bright sunlight and the fresh smells. "It's beautiful up here." I looked all around at the green foliage and pointed to a handful of deer who were having their breakfast in a field at the side of the road. "Deer!"

"Yes, you'll see plenty of them up here. They come right into the yard. My mother used to take tons of pictures of them when they first bought the place. Now, we're pretty used to them." He took a turn, and we headed into an upscale neighborhood, full of mansions.

My nerves kicked in as I realized we were almost there. "Is it silly of me to think some of these people will look down their noses at me?"

"If they do, I'll straighten them out. It doesn't matter where you came from, it matters that you're my wife. You'll be treated with respect or the person or persons who fail to do so will feel my wrath." He took my hand and kissed it. "I don't want you to worry about a thing."

I nodded but knew he wouldn't always be right by my side to protect me from people I knew could be hateful. Jett had told me about his mother wanting to set him up with rich single women who lived in the area. That's when he first came up with the wife lie so he wouldn't have to go through the torture of being set up.

My woman's intuition told me not to expect a warm welcome. His parents might be nice, they were when I met them that first day, but it was doubtful that anyone else would be half as nice as they were.

The gate was open when we got to it. There was a long and winding driveway that led up to the three-storey, light blue, art deco style mansion. Each section of the home was like a huge block, and giant windows were in each one of them, overlooking the rolling hills that made up the estate.

Shrubs were manicured into the shapes of deer, squirrels and swans. It was neat, extravagant, and looked like something out of a magazine. "Wow, Jett. That's all I can say. This is where we'll be spending the week?"

"This is it, my parent's summer home." He pulled around the home to the back where there was an enormous garage. "As you can see, it's set up for multiple guests. There are no less than fifteen bedrooms, all with private baths. Five living areas, three dining areas, a gym, and an indoor, outdoor pool area, as well as a game room, or course."

"Of course," I had to laugh. "One can't have a proper vacation house without that," I used a snooty New York accent that made him laugh.

"Careful now, you'll meet quite a few people here with that accent."

A man came out of a door at the end of the garage, and one of the doors opened. He waved us in, and we parked next to a Rolls Royce.

"Your parent's?"

"My grandparent's. Dad bought his father that car last year. Neither set of my grandparents allow too much to be lavished upon them, but they all did take cars, and they do take the week long vacation once a year here and another one in Wyoming in the spring. That vacation isn't as socially intense as this one is."

I thought about Wyoming in the spring and it kind of hurt that I wouldn't get to be a part of that. We'd be over by then.

"So the summer is spent here, and the rest of the year this place is closed up or what?" The man who'd opened the garage door for us was suddenly at my door, opening it for me.

"Mrs. Simmons, how nice to make your acquaintance. I am Rock, the keeper of the cars." He held out his hand, and I gave it a shake.

"Nice to meet you, Rock, keeper of the cars. And it looks like you have some very nice ones to keep, don't you?"

He nodded and smiled. "That I do. All summer long, I get to clean, gas up, and take for routine maintenance some very nice vehicles."

Jett's hand took mine as he looked at Rock over his shoulder. "Be gentle with her, she's brand new. No maintenance needed this week. But she could use some gas." We walked away at a quick pace.

"You should've started that with a hello to the elderly man, Jett," I scolded him.

That stopped him in his tracks as he looked at me with wide eyes. "What did you say to me?"

For a moment I felt like I'd done something wrong. Then I jutted out my jaw. "I said, you should've said hello first. That was rude of you not to do that."

He eyed me for a long moment then looked past me at Rock. "How's the wife, Rock?"

"She's doing fine, Mr. Simmons."

"Glad to hear it. And you? How've you been?"

"Fine, just fine, sir. Thanks for asking."

"You have a good day, Rock. It's always a pleasure to see you." Jett looked back at me and whispered. "Did that satisfy you, my dear?"

With a nod, I began to walk again. "It did, actually."

He laughed and smacked my ass. "You have moxie, my little Asia. I have to give you that."

We went into the house through a side door that looked like it might be a mudroom. Raincoats hung on hooks, galoshes of different colors and sizes were in a row on a shelf, and there were umbrellas in a stand. We walked through that room and into a state-of-the-art kitchen where three women in white uniforms were busily preparing lunch.

Jett was breezy with them, "Hi all, how's it going this fine day?"

"Fine, Mr. Simmons," one of them said as she gave him a nod. "And this must be the wife we've been hearing your parents talk about." The woman, who looked like she was in charge of the others, wiped her hands on a white towel that hung off her white apron. She came to me, and we shook hands. "I'm Cora, the Simmons' chef." She pointed to a short dark haired woman. "That's Tanya, and the other one is Mary. If you have any dietary concerns or allergies, you let me know."

"None that I know of." I shook my head. "Nice to meet you all." I found her nice and helpful too. So far, so good. But then again, I'd only met the staff. They were expected to be cordial to me. The guests wouldn't be.

"The family is in the solarium, soaking up the morning sun," she informed us before she got back to work.

We left the kitchen, walked through a dining area with a bright white long table and chairs set. "This is one of the informal dining areas," Jett said as we walked through it. The next room was a bar. "You can see what this room is."

"Yes, it's fairly obvious. The large, ornately carved wooden bar tells it all."

He let go of my hand and went behind it. "Might as well mix up a couple of drinks while we're here. It'll help take the edge off what's about to happen. We'll be faced with tons of questions when we get in there."

I took a seat on one of the bar stools. Although it was way too early for me, I didn't say a word. If Jett wanted a drink this early, it meant we were in for it, and I wasn't about to argue with him about it. Filling two tall glasses with ice, he poured bourbon in his, filling it hallway up. He was looking to calm some nerves alright! He finished it off with some soda. Then he found some rum, though is wasn't coconut and wiggled the bottle at me. "Rum and lemon lime soda, or something else?"

"Can I have what you're having, but only about half as much liquor?"

With a nod, he fixed me up and then we each took drinks. It wasn't magic, and it didn't soothe my nerves, but I knew in time it would help. He extended his arm. "You ready?"

"No." I gave him a smile. "But I'll pretend to be."

"That's all I can ask."

Into the solarium, we went, where things were about to get real!

# 19

# JETT

The time was at hand to lie again. My fake marriage had been going great, but could we pull it off with my whole family in the front row seats?

The whiskey hadn't had time to set in and do its job, but I had hopes it'd soon kick in. I had Asia by the hand as we strode into the large, glass enclosed room.

Lounging around the area that was filled with chaise longues were both sets of my grandparents, my parents, and some woman I'd never met. A tall woman with long legs that extended out from under a pair of white shorts. High heeled, strappy sandals ended those long legs, and when I got up to her face, I found her smiling at me. She got up and came right to us. "You must be the happy new couple."

I shook her hand as she gazed at me. "We are them. Mr. and Mrs. Simmons. I'm Jett, she's Asia. And you are?"

"I'm Janice Duncan. Your mother hired me to plan your coming out as a married couple party."

"It's nice to meet you, Janice." Asia shook her hand. "But we don't need a party."

"Nonsense," my mother said as she got up to come to us. "And I have another surprise for you two. We'll make that announcement at your party, though. You'll just have to wait for that one." Mom took Asia by the hand. "Come with us, my dear. Jett isn't into party planning. You, me and Janice will do all that."

As I watched Asia get taken away, I felt panicky for a moment. "Wait!" They all three stopped and turned to look at me. "I want to introduce her to my grandparents, Mom."

"Oh." Mom looked a bit ashamed. "Allow me to do that." She whisked Asia off to meet my mother's parents then she hurriedly made an introduction to my father's parents before she, my fake wife, and the party planner were gone.

I was alone. Well, not entirely. That would've been so much better.

"Come, boy," my father's father called out as my dad and grandparents moved to form a circle at which I was the center. "Now tell us how you went about marrying a girl you barely know."

"And we want to meet her family, Jett." Grandmother Shapiro, my mother's mother, didn't look like she'd be put off about that.

"Oh, I don't think they could make it. They have work. Her mother works at a law firm. Her father… well, I'm sure he's busy too." Her father was out of work, is what she'd told me. I didn't know if Asia wanted everyone to know that or not.

"They could come for the weekend, at the very least." Dad was pretty intent on getting them to come. "I can send a car for them. We really should meet them. They're your family too now. That makes them ours too."

The sentiment was sweet, but the lie of a marriage made it a stupid thing to do. Her parent's involvement wasn't part of the plan. I couldn't ask her to go to those lengths for me.

Grandmother Simmons patted the empty space next to her. "Come, Jett. Sit down and tell us all about your whirlwind romance that left you hitched."

It was funny, without Asia at my side, I kind of forgot our little story. I took a seat. "We like to tell our story together. I'll wait for her."

"Nonsense." Grandmother Simmons wasn't taking no for an answer. "How'd you know she was the one, Jett. After all this time. How did you know?"

"First of all, I am not some old man. I'm twenty-six. Why does everyone in this family act like that's too old to be single?"

"It's your lifestyle, son. I've told you this." Dad shook his head as if that answer alone justified how they thought.

"Is it some kind of lust-filled attraction, Jett?" Grandfather Shapiro asked me. "Because those kinds of relationships never last."

"No, no, it's nothing like that. We have a lot of things in common. We like the same things, think along the same lines, mostly. I never feel alone. Even when we're not right next to each other, I feel like I'm a part of her. It's odd, but in a great way." The funny thing about me saying that, is that it was completely true. I just hadn't thought about it before.

Both my grandmothers' white heads bobbed as they agreed with me. Then Grandfather Simmons popped off, "And is the sex hot? I mean it needs to be hot in the beginning. Every couple needs a thread of passion that connects them too, you know."

I felt heat flush my face. "Yes, sir. We have hot sex." And just as I said that my mother and fake wife were back in the room and both had gaping mouths.

Asia went scarlet. "Jett!"

I hopped up and hurried to her. "Baby, you have no idea the questions they've been asking. I didn't mean to say that. I swear it!"

The set of rogues who had me saying such a thing got a nice long glare from my mother. "Okay, you nosey lot. Let's leave these two alone for a bit. I think we're overwhelming them." Mom kissed my cheek. "I've had Rock take your things to the Monte Carlo Suite. Show Asia your bedroom and then you two can come back down whenever you're ready to."

Draping my arm around Asia's shoulders, I took my fake wife and headed out of the sunny room full of my closest relatives. If they were that tough, what would the rest of them be like?

Heading to the back staircase, I led Asia up two flights of stairs to the third floor where the Monte Carlo Suite was located. "Mom's named all the rooms. I suppose she gave us this one because we said we got married in Vegas. It's got a gambling theme to it."

When I opened the door, and we went inside, I guess Asia felt like it was finally safe to talk. “Oh, God, Jett. They want my parents to come!”

“Yeah, I know. Don’t worry, I’ll make something up.” I went over to the bar that was in the room and looked for something to make another drink. Mine had been lost in the solarium, and Asia’s was gone too.

“Your mother wants my parent’s phone number. She wants to call and invite them herself. She asked if we’d gone to introduce you to them and I didn’t know what the hell to say, Jett. It was like I had a mouthful of gum. I mumbled, yes. I’m an idiot! How are we going to fix that lie? This is too much!”

“Calm down!” I wasn’t finding what I wanted. There were wine and spritzers, waters, sodas, but no Goddamn whiskey of any kind in that bar. “What kind of fucking bar is this?”

“And what’s up with the drinking, Jett? You don’t drink like this. Are you planning on staying lit up this entire week?” She shook her head and fell back on the bed.

“I wasn’t planning on it, but now that I’ve seen what it’s going to be like, I might just stay drunk. Want to join me?”

She laughed then. A crazy, maniacal sound that had me joining in. “This is crazy, Jett!”

“I know!”

I fell onto the bed beside her then rolled over and pulled her to face me. “Thank you for being here. I know I paid you to, but thank you for trying so hard to make this work for me. Perhaps we could hire some people to play the role of your parents.”

She laughed and smiled. “How I wish we could, Jett. I’ve really fucked it all up. Your mother made me show her pictures of my family. She was certain I had some on my cell, and I didn’t know what else to do. She’s seen their faces. I told you I’m a terrible liar.”

I blinked as I stared into her eyes. “You know what I think will make us both chill the fuck out?”

“Morphine?”

I ran my hand up her silky thigh until I came to the edge of her khaki shorts. “No, a little love making should clear our heads and help us think.”

“I agree.” She ran her hand over my cheek. “And I’d like to try out my skills on you to help you relax.”

“Your skills?”

She nodded. “I practiced fellatio on a cucumber before I met you. Wanna let me give it a shot on you?”

Well, who the hell says no to that?

# 20

# ASIA

The crystal chandelier made Jett's eyes sparkle as they caught all the tiny sparkles of light refracting. He'd made sure to please me every time we'd been intimate. I had no one to compare Jett to, but I thought he was a selfless lover. He always thought about me and how I was feeling, what made me feel good, what made me happy.

It was time I got to do something for him. As far as being a Dom went, I didn't think he was much of one. I did ask what he did with his other subs. He told me, he mostly wanted them to be quiet, do as he said, he hadn't talked to them much. He admitted to treating me nothing like he treated any of them.

When I asked him why he thought that might be, he said it was probably because he had another agenda with me, the fake marriage thing. Jett had a definite idea of what kind of relationship he thought marriage was.

Respect was mutual. All things were shared. And you knew, no matter what, that you could depend on each other through thick and thin. He explained how hard it was to take women seriously when you have a lot of money. Many only want your money. It can and had, made Jett a man who trusted no one.

Except me. He was beginning to trust me. Without even trying, I'd managed to earn some of his trust. I wasn't sure how I'd even accomplished that. But I was glad I had.

Jett was exceptional. I didn't know the man he said he was, I only knew who he was with me. That man was kind, considerate, and loving. That man was the kind of man a woman could really fall in love with. Trust with her life. And I was doing all of that.

He piled the pillows behind his head as I eased up from the end of the bed. Unbuckling his belt, I went for the button next, unzipped the zipper of his khaki shorts that cutely matched mine, and gently took out his half engorged cock.

One kiss to the top had him gathering my hair in his hands to pull it out of the way. "I wanna watch."

I smiled then ran my hands up and down his long length and placed my lips at the top. Opening my mouth, I used my lips to sheath my teeth and moved down his silky dick. The deep moan he made had me feeling like he was happy with my technique, a thing I was a little worried about.

When I'd searched the internet for how to give a great blowjob, I found many had the same opinion. As long as you don't bite or scratch with your teeth, there really was no way to give a bad one!

As I went up and down, he grew and grew, going deeper down my throat. "Oh, baby… you're taking me like a pro. Damn, are you even real?"

I was very real, and I had high hopes he'd come to see what we had wasn't made up. It may have started that way, but we were building something that was very real. If only he'd see that and stop pretending we were married, we might be able to grow as a couple, instead of the fake marriage scam he had going on.

He moved my head faster. "Oh, baby, I'm almost there. Wanna try to swallow?" I hummed a yes, and he understood. "Oh, God! Hum some more. Shit! You're incredible, baby!"

Only a few more strokes then I moved one hand to fondle his balls, and he was shooting cum down my throat. It went so quickly, it went down smoothly. I was pleased with myself and licked him clean as he groaned.

"So that was alright then?" He answered with a nod as his eyes were closed and he was deeply relaxed.

I got up and went to the bathroom, finding my toiletry bag had already been put on the long vanity with double sinks. Finding my toothbrush, I set about cleaning my mouth up because let's face it, what guy wants to taste their own cum?

I'd just rinsed my mouth when Jett threw open the door, butt naked and began to undress me at a frantic speed. Then he turned me around and made me face the mirror. He pushed the top half of me down on the vanity and thrust into my ass. I moaned and gasped at the same time, "Yes!"

Jett had messed with my ass a lot but hadn't gotten his cock all the way into it. It burned nearly the same way as when he first put his cock into my vagina. Just like that burn, I liked it.

I could watch in the mirror as he fucked me. And he watched himself too. His eyes were glued to our bodies, mine were glued to him. His muscles and how they rippled, made me hot. Sweat was making his skin shiny, and his long hair clung to his face.

At that moment, I felt like he was in Dom mode. Taking what he wanted and not wanting to talk about it. There was a fire in his eyes that hadn't been there before.

Somewhere inside of me, I was telling myself I should be afraid. The Jett I knew might be retreating and the Dom he really was, was coming forth.

Could I handle the next few months with a real Dom?

Perhaps the blowjob had been a mistake. Perhaps I'd been just like all the rest of the subs he'd had, and it sullied me in his eyes somehow. Whatever had happened, it didn't matter. Because I loved this version of Jett too!

He was all man. And as brutal as he seemed, I was taking it. Enjoying it as much as he was. Jett could treat me any way he wanted to. As long he was with me, that's all that mattered.

Suddenly, he pulled out of me and lifted me up, turned me around and put me up against the wall. I wrapped my legs around him as he forced his cock into me. His mouth crashed onto mine, forcing his tongue further into my mouth than he ever had. Everything he was doing was intended to be forceful and invasive, I could tell that, instinctively.

Was the honeymoon over?

Did I care if it was?

Making love was great, and I thought we'd do that more, but this fucking stuff was hotter than hell!

His mouth left mine and went to my neck. He tortured it with bites then pulled it as he sucked it. I ran my hands over the bulging muscles of his back, as I tried not to scream with desire. If we'd been in our home, I'd have raised the roof with animal-like howls. He was turning me into a wild woman. And I was loving every moment of the transformation.

He wrapped his arms around me, pulling me away from the wall and carrying me to the shower. "Turn it on," he growled at me.

I reached around him and grabbed the knob, turning it to warm. The water fell down on us like a warm summer rain as he pushed my back up against the cool tiled wall and savagely pummeled me once more. Our breaths echoed in the shower, making me even more aroused by the sounds of us together in that state of erotica. My body couldn't take any more, I couldn't hold it back, even though I really wanted it to last longer. I cried out as I came. He made only a few more hard thrusts before he lost his load too. The sound he made was as if he was a werewolf who'd been shot by a silver bullet, it was so beastly.

I was shaking. Tears ran down my cheeks. Not from fear or that I was hurt. I had no real clue why that was happening.

He let me go and pulled back, finding me in that odd state. "I'm okay Jett. I am."

His lips curled into a sinister grin. "I know you are. The tears are from the intensity. Fucking is intense. Making love is a softer version that doesn't usually evoke such emotions. You did well. Better than expected, since I came at you without giving you any idea about what I was going to do."

"Thank you for being who you really are with me, Jett." I ran my hands through his hair. "Can I wash your hair for you?"

He nodded as he gazed at me. "I don't deserve you, Asia. You're perfect. How the hell did you turn out so damn perfect?"

"I'm far from perfect." I filled my hand with a spicy smelling shampoo then massaged it into his thick dark hair.

He put his finger to my lips. "I am the Dom, I tell you what you are and what you aren't. You are my perfect little Asia, and you always will be."

A shudder ran through me. Did he mean the end of the contract wouldn't end us? Should I dare to ask?

Things were going so well, I decided not to say anything more than, "I am yours. For as long as you want me."

His lips grazed mine. "Good girl."

My heart pounded with desire once more. Would we ever get out of that bedroom and down to deal with the people he brought me to lie to for him?

## 21

## JETT

Feeling fresh, Asia and I headed down to face my family. We had the story on her family straight. They were headed to see her sister because the baby was about to be due. We'd have them all over for dinner once they got back, which would be a few weeks. A thing that would never transpire.

With our story set, we found everyone heading into one of the dining rooms where lunch was being served. I ran my arm around Asia and pulled her in tight to my side, then kissed the side of her head. "Good, I'm starving."

"Me too." She put her hand on my chest and looked up at me. "Tarzan."

I made a little growl and felt like the master of my domain where she was concerned. I'd given into my wild side. I couldn't hold back any longer. Asia had gotten two weeks with the softer side of me that no one else had ever had before. It was time she got to know the beast that resided within me. And how pleasantly surprised I was that she was completely into it all. She thrived as I took her the way I'd dreamt of doing.

My little Asia was more than I ever expected. And we had just begun to test our limits. What would the future hold for us?

Would two and a half months more be enough for me? And if it wasn't, would Asia really want to continue without a contract? Or would she only stay with me if we had another contract and I paid her more for doing it?

I'd always had the idea that women wanted me for my money. I had no idea if I'd keep feeling the same way about Asia if she only wanted to continue things with me if we had another contract and more money. If that happened, then I'd know she'd just been acting the entire time.

That would hurt, a thing I didn't allow to happen to me. At least I'd know I'd been duped by the lovely little creature. I could move on from her then. But I hoped like hell that wasn't the case.

As we entered the dining room, I saw a few more people had arrived. Uncle Pete was sitting at the end of the long table, Aunt Sally sat at his right, and their twins, Bo and Joe were seated across from them.

Mom stood up, waving everyone into the room. "The place cards have everyone's names on them. Please, take your seats. Chef Cora has made us a wonderful meal of ceviche as our first course, Grilled salmon for the main, served on a bed of asparagus and wild rice." She looked directly at Asia as we filed in. "Doesn't that sound delicious, Asia?"

"Yes, ma'am, it does. Is there a dessert too?"

"Oh, my, yes. Of course, there's a dessert. Tell me, have you ever had key lime pie before?" Mom licked her pink stained lips.

Asia shook her head. "No, I've never had it. It sounds yummy, though."

Mom clapped her thin hands as she smiled at the woman she thought was my wife. "It is yummy!" She pointed to the front of the table. "That's you two, dear. I want my kids right next to me."

As she used the term, her kids, it sent a jolt of pure, unadulterated guilt right to my heart. I was bringing in a woman my mother would get close to, under false pretenses. The lie went to new levels of heavy as it weighed not so much on my shoulders as inside my heart.

Asia gripped my hand as we went to where my mother had pointed and looked at me with a smile. But I saw the guilt behind her eyes too. It was wrong what I was doing. We both felt it.

But what could I do about it now?

I wasn't about to break down and admit things on the first day of the vacation. That would mean pure hell for me. No, we would stick with the lie, no matter how much guilt piled up on us.

I was paying Asia extremely well to maintain what I needed from her. She'd take the guilt right along with me. It was her job to do that. It just kinda sucked donkey dicks that doing that to Asia also added to my guilt, doubling my load.

Dad was sitting at the head of the table, Mom to his right and Asia, then me to his left. It was the first time I'd ever had a woman with me at any family gathering. It felt nice.

Aunt Sally waved at us from the other end of the long table. "Hi there. After lunch, I'm dying to get to know you, Asia."

"Asia, meet my Aunt Sally, my mother's sister." I gave my aunt a nod. "The man at the other end of the table is her husband, Pete, and the two little redheads that are sitting across from her are their ten-year-old twins, Bo and Joe."

Asia gave a wave back. "I'll be sure to find you after lunch, Aunt Sally."

And there it was again, the guilt shot, going right into my heart again. Asia had called her Aunt. It was a lot to take. Then Mom took her seat across from us and extended her hand across the table to Asia. The two clasped hands. "Dear, it would be the greatest honor to me, and Jett's father is you'd call us, Mom and Dad."

Oh, that was it!

I couldn't take it anymore! "Mom, she has a Mom and Dad. I think her parents might just hate it if she did that. Don't ask her to do that. She can call you two by your first names."

Mom's eyes slanted as she looked sad. "Oh, Jett, I don't mean to step on her parents' toes. It's just that I've always wanted a daughter, you know that. If I could hear her sweet voice, calling me, Mom and your father, Dad, then it would make my life, son. You have no idea. Please, don't take that away from me."

For the love of Pete!

I looked at Asia. "Is that something you'd be comfortable with, baby?"

She searched my eyes for what I wanted her to say. But then I guess she read me wrong. She turned her eyes to my mother. "I'd love to call you two Mom and Dad. Thank you for that honor, Mom."

And there it was, my fake wife was now calling my parents endearing terms and I was getting in even deeper. The walls of the cave of lies were starting to get thicker and seemed to be depriving me of oxygen. How long would there be enough air to breathe?

The first course was brought out, along with white wine and water. I leaned over to whisper, "You don't have to drink the wine, baby. I know you don't like it."

"I'll drink it, Jett. I don't want to be rude. It doesn't bother me. It's just not my favorite drink is all."

"I don't want you to do anything you don't want to. Don't drink it."

She looked at me with an odd expression. "Are you telling me not to drink it when I told you I don't mind and find it to be rude if I don't?"

I nodded. "Do as I say, Asia."

She jutted out her jaw, defiantly and picked up her wine glass, taking a sip. "Yum." She looked at my mother. "This is delicious, great choice, Mom" She licked her ruby red lips. "You should taste it, honey. It's great."

And there it was. The first time she went against a direct order. Asia would soon find out what it meant to be a sub. I had no choice but to teach her a lesson about defying me!

# 22

# ASIA

Everyone in Jett's family was nice as they could be to me. I thought it was all going great, except for how Jett was acting. He was growing sullen and became quiet. It was as if he didn't want us all to get along. Perhaps he thought there'd be more strife between us for some reason. Whatever it was, it was beginning to annoy me.

Sitting by the pool, his twin cousins jumped in right by us, splashing us and giving us a good dousing. Jett stood up. "Damn it, you two!" He took my hand, and off we went, back into the house.

I followed along without saying a word. He was overreacting to something so benign. When we got into the house, I found him taking me up a back set of stairs and then into our bedroom.

When he turned around to face me, closing the door behind us, I saw something in his eyes I hadn't before. Anger. "Asia, would you like to explain to me why you think it's okay for you to defy me?"

"What are you talking about?" I was at a loss as to what his main malfunction was.

"The wine, Asia. I told you not to drink it, and you did anyway." He walked away from me and went to sit on the bed. "I won't have you disregarding me. Come here, it's time for your first punishment."

Standing still, I put my hands on my hips. "Do you think for one damn minute that I'm going to come to you, bend over your lap so you can spank me, over that?"

He nodded. "You're my sub, Asia. I told you not to do anything you didn't want to do."

"I wanted to drink the fucking wine, jackass!" I stomped my foot.

His face went red. "Do not cuss at me or call me names, sub." He stood up and pointed to the floor. "On your knees, now!"

Looking at him, I could see he was beyond angry. But it wasn't because I drank the wine. And I wasn't about to fall on my knees.

"Jett, tell me what the real problem is. This isn't about the wine. You can talk to me." I took a step forward and eased up to him as he shook with anger. "Sweetie, you can tell me anything."

He was gritting his teeth and shaking his head. "Why are you not doing as I told you to, sub?"

"Because you are not punishing me for drinking the wine. Something else is bothering you, and I want to help you deal with that. Is it about me calling your parents Mom and Dad?"

He spun around and huffed then sat on the bed and put his face in his hands. "Fuck! Asia, God damn it! Are you insane? Do you know what any other Dom would be doing to you right now for how contrary you're being?"

I eased up to him and ran my hand over his head, gently soothing him. "I do. But you're not an ordinary Dom. And I didn't do anything wrong. You told me not to do anything I didn't want to. I wanted to drink the wine. I didn't disobey you, and now I know what really set you off. You don't like how well your family and I are getting along."

He looked up at me, and I could see it all in his sea green eyes. Guilt! "Asia, I didn't expect all of this. I didn't know they'd all love you. How did you do that so quickly?" He shook his head and looked distraught. "How will I ever get them to understand things when we end this?"

And there it was. He was planning on letting me go once the contract was up. He was worried about how his family would react to the phony divorce.

"My poor Jett. You didn't think this thing all the way through. I thought as much." I cupped his face in my hands. "Don't worry so much about what will happen in the future. Your family will be a bit upset by it, but you can blame me for the divorce. You can say you caught me with an old boyfriend, messing around on you. They'll hate me and be there to comfort you."

He ran his hands up the backs of my legs, sending chills through me. "Asia, what did I ever to do deserve you?"

"You paid a shit-ton of money, is what you did." I smiled at him. "Can we go back down and act like a happy couple now. I hate fighting with you."

"Wanna know something?" He grinned at me as I nodded. "You're the only woman I've ever actually argued with. I've never cared enough about anyone to actually hear them out. What've you done to me, Asia Jones?"

I ran my arms around his neck and leaned in to whisper in his ear, "I've put a spell on you, Jett Simmons."

He picked me up and sat me on his lap as he ran his hand through my hair. "That, you have, my little Asia." He pulled me back, and our lips met.

I'd never made up after a fight before, his kiss was apologetic. Soft, caressing, and it told me he was sorry. More so than his words did. His hands grazed my shoulders and back as the kiss grew, gaining intensity.

He eased back, lying on the bed. I moved my body to straddle his. Maybe another round of wild sex would settle his guilt. I was up for anything!

I moved my body over his and felt his cock rising under his bathing suit. I had on a bikini with a thin lace cover up over it. His hand moved between us, pushing the top of his bathing suit down then easing my bikini bottoms to the side. He picked me up and slid me down onto his erection.

"Baby, fuck you feel so good," he moaned as he released my lips.

We looked into each other's eyes as he lifted me up and down at a slow speed. "When you're inside of me, I feel like a part of you, Jett. Is that normal?"

"I don't think any of this is normal, Asia. Not one bit of it."

I kissed him again, letting that sink in. What we had wasn't normal. I'd never had anything, so I had to go on what he said. But then again, Jett had never had anything more than sex with women, either.

The word, love, kept going through my head. I was pretty sure we'd found it. But I had no idea what he'd do with the love we shared.

I could see it more clearly then. Jett was fighting himself about how he felt about me. There was something in the back of his mind that had him either on the fence about me or on the fence about love, in general.

Jett's hands moved off my waist, and he pushed me up. I rode him and ran my hands over his bare chest as he ran his hands up to push my top up to fondle my breasts. "Asia, is this real? Can I trust you?"

"You can trust me. I'm not faking anything. Is that a concern you have about me? I'm not a trained sub. I don't know how to act as if I care for anyone. I'm not a liar, although I'm becoming better at it since we came here."

His face fell, he looked sad. "I'm sorry about all that. I am. I think one of the reasons I got so mad was because I'm mad at myself for doing this to you and my family. And I have no idea how the hell I'm going to make things right for any of you."

I took a deep breath to try to find an answer to his dilemma. I couldn't find one. "Jett, just let things play out. You'll know what the right thing is to do when the times comes. You'll see."

He caressed my cheek then rolled over with me, making gentle strokes as he looked down at me. "As a sub, you suck, Asia. As a wife, you rock my world."

I wasn't sure how to take that. I'd signed up to be his sub, not his wife. Neither was a role I'd ever played or even thought much about playing. Jett came into my life and turned it upside down. In both good and bad ways.

All I knew for sure was that this man would leave his mark on me. He'd forever have a place in my heart and head no man would ever be able to erase.

## 23

# JETT

With Asia at my side, I began to feel better about things. The guilt was still there, but it was a weight I was getting used to. And when the neighbors came for a little dinner party on the fourth night there, I remembered exactly why I had a fake wife in the first place.

My mother, the matchmaker!

Five, very eligible rich bitches had come with their old-money families to Mom's soiree. Three of them were tall, elegant, and snooty, two were short, chunky, and insecure. All three were green with envy about Asia. None of them were nice to her. A thing that was pissing me off to no end.

Madison of the Greenberg family was the biggest bitch of all. One of the tall women, she kind of overshadowed them all. With her hands on her skinny hips, she looked Asia up and down as I came outside, finding the five had surrounded my little fake wife. "And where is it you came from? And how did you manage to get one of the most eligible bachelors into your claws, you little thing?"

Asia looked up at the giraffe of a woman. "Um, uh, he and I met in Los Angeles while I was on vacation there. It was love at first sight."

There were many people at the party. I was having difficulty getting to the group as I had to zigzag through the crowd, and many stopped me, asking me how married life was. My answers were short and to the point, "Great, gotta get to my wife now."

The gaggle of women all laughed as if what Asia had said could never be true. One of the short women said, "I don't see how that happened. You're nowhere near the league of woman, Jett Simmons needs in his life. How're you supposed to help him in polite society?"

I stepped up, reaching through one short and one tall woman. Grabbing Asia by the arm, I pulled her out of the mean circle. "Baby, there you are."

Asia looked a little wide-eyed. "I'm right here, honey."

The five women looked me over as I ran my arm, protectively around Asia's waist and kissed her cheek. The tallest and meanest of them all, Madison, sneered directly at Asia before she smiled at me. "Jett, my father's having a charity ball in the fall. I know you're married now, but do you suppose you could accompany me to it? You wouldn't mind, would you, Asia? It is for charity. The wealthy patrons will expect me to have a man of their stature as my date. I've planned on asking Jett for months now, waiting for this chance to ask him. Surely, you have enough security in your marriage to let your husband take me to such a function, Asia."

Not waiting for Asia to answer that, I said, "I'm sorry about that, Madison. I'm not about to go out with another woman. My wife can't answer that for me."

"But I need you, Jett." Madison made a sultry frown. "Can't you help me out?"

"What's the problem, Madison?" Asia asked. "Can't you find a single man to ask to the ball? Or have you gone through all the eligible men around here?"

The women gave Asia shitty looks. My poor Asia was out of her league with the bitches. They'd been bred to be bitchy!

"Come, Asia, we have other guests to greet." I turned her around, feeling the cold stares of the women as we walked away. I kissed the side of her head. "Baby, you gave it your best shot, but those women would've eaten you alive. Best to stay right next to me for the remainder of the night."

"Oh, they weren't so bad. I was handling them." She laughed and placed her hand on my chest, then gave my lips a quick peck. "But thank you for getting me out of the ring of fire they had me in. I was wondering if I'd have to drop and crawl out of them."

Janice Duncan, the party planner, popped out of the crowd in front of us. "Hello, you two! Are you getting excited for your party this weekend?"

I was anything but excited. "Oh, I'd forgotten about that whole thing."

Asia gave me a scowl. "He's kidding, Janice. Of course, we're excited. Neither of us can wait to see what you've come up with."

Janice smiled and shook her head. "Jett, you rascal. On Friday the clothes you two are to wear will be brought over. Your mother gave me the sizes. It's going to be fancy. You'll see that when the things arrive. We want to give your marriage a great start. And East Coast royalty will be there to bring you into their fold. I know you'll love it." She looked over her shoulder as some man said something about his daughter turning sixteen next month. "I'll see you guys later." Off she went to cash in on another party, and I took my fake wife to the dance floor.

"It looks like you're going to the dance floor, Jett. I actually can't dance. I've never danced at all." Asia looked worried as she watched the other couples dancing around the floor my mother had brought in for her party. A small, three piece band played on a temporary stage at one end of it.

"We'll be expected to dance at our party. May as well learn now." I found a dark corner and held her tightly. "Feel my feet right next to yours?" I placed one leg between hers and made sure our feet were touching.

"I do." She looked nervous, and it made me chuckle.

"It's just dancing, baby. Nothing to fear." I moved one foot. "Let your feet follow mine. I won't make any fancy movements. I'll keep it very simple."

"I'll try not to step on your toes." She moved her foot alongside mine.

"That's right, keep your feet on the floor, don't lift them, slide them.

It's easy, see?" I slid mine and hers slid along with them. Before she knew it, we were dancing across the floor. "You're a fast learner, Asia." She smiled then rested her head on my shoulder. "My body seems to follow yours in every way, Jett."

It did too. We were so compatible it wasn't even funny. Where I ended, she began. We moved all over that dance floor. I got fancy with my footwork, and she effortlessly followed along. When the song ended, we found people had stopped dancing to watch us, and everyone clapped.

"Oh, goodness!" Asia blushed, furiously and buried her head in my chest. "Everyone was watching us, Jett!"

"And you did a fantastic job, baby. Now let's take a bow." I moved her out beside me, and she followed along, bowing to our supportive audience. "Thank you, thank you."

I led Asia off the wooden floor and found one man in particular, looking my fake wife up and down. Asia was wearing a thin, silk, dark blue dress and black flats. Her hair was pulled back into a sleek up-do. She looked radiant, and the blush on her cheeks only served to make her even more beautiful. The young man's hand came out, and he had Asia's in his before I knew what had happened. "Excuse me, I'm Sebastien Greenberg. I wanted to introduce myself, Asia. It seems Jett here has found himself a little slice of Heaven. Are there more at home like you?"

Asia smiled at him. "Nice to meet you and no, my sisters are married, Sebastien."

I didn't recall knowing the man. "Sebastien? Oh, wait, didn't you just graduate from high school?"

His dark eyes lingered on Asia. "College, Jett. I just graduated from Harvard Law School." He looked at me. "Mind if I take your wife for a little spin on the dance floor? I promise I'll bring her right back to you."

Asia looked up at me with worried eyes. I knew she didn't want to tell the man that was the first time she'd danced. And I also didn't want to see another man holding her. "Sorry, she and I were about to get a drink. Maybe another time, Sebastien." I ran my hand off Asia's waist, and took her hand, then walked away from the man who was looking at my woman much too hard.

"Thank you, Jett," Asia whispered. "I was afraid etiquette would force you to allow him to dance with me."

"Normally, it would. But this is an abnormal situation we're in." We stopped at the first bar. "Two screwdrivers, please." I took her chin between my thumb and forefinger. "Everything about you and I is abnormal. I can't think of seeing you in any other man's arms. You evoke jealousy in me. Now, why do you suppose that is?"

"I don't know, Jett." She grinned, crookedly. "Perhaps you're falling in love with me."

All I could do was stare into her doe-like eyes. "You think so, huh? And how about you? Are you falling in love with me, my little Asia?" The bartender placed our drinks on the bar, and I took one, handing it to her then picked up mine and tapped our glasses together. Asia took a sip as I did, then her eyes twinkled. "Maybe I am, Jett Simmons. What do you think about that?"

I thought that was the most frightening thing I'd ever heard!

Love, with a sub?

What had I gotten myself into?

## 24

# ASIA

The night of our party was at hand. Janice had me in a flowing white dress that went to the floor. High heels were hidden beneath the layers of gossamer. Jett was clad in a tuxedo, making him look like the groom he was pretending to be. Everyone stood and cheered as they clapped when we made our grand entrance into the ballroom at a fancy hotel nearby.

It was all a bit on the uppity side for me. I couldn't say I wasn't impressed because I was. But it wasn't me. I didn't feel like me at all. I felt like another person. A person who was vain and mostly empty inside.

But I went through the motions for Jett's mother. The woman was dead set on being a part of the wealthy society, she'd only gained a place in once they'd made their little bakery into a billion dollar business.

Zane bowed, and I did what he did, then the band started playing, and he and I danced as they all watched. I had to close my eyes and lay my head on his shoulder. This wasn't who I was.

Somehow, in the hurried pace of things, I'd lost the Asia I'd been. I was wearing expensive clothes, riding in luxurious cars, the likes I'd never known before, and eating foods I didn't know existed.

The only thing that was true about me was how I felt with Jett. I felt at home with him at all times. That's what kept me going. He needed me to portray a particular type of woman, and I did that for him.

After the dance, his mother and father took the stage. Jett and I stood on the dance floor and looked up at them as his father took the mic.

"Jett and Asia, how good it is to see you both so happy. As you know, your mother and I told you that we had a surprise for you. And the time has come to give it to you."

His mother took the mic. "Asia, you're the most remarkable woman I've ever had the pleasure of meeting. With your influence, our son has blossomed into the man we always knew he could be, with the right woman at his side. We adore you." Applause rang out as my cheeks heated with embarrassment.

When I looked at Jett, I found his cheeks were red too. He leaned in to whisper, "God, I'm sorry about this, Asia."

I nodded in understanding. Things had gotten way out of hand. If only Jett had thought things through, all of this hoopla wouldn't be happening. But it was, and things just kept going on and on.

His father took over. "It's no secret that I've wanted to rest for quite some time. And now that Jett is ready and settled, the time has come for him to take over my job as CEO of Sin-a-buns Sweetshop."

Jett's jaw hung open as applause thundered through the large ballroom. I turned to hug Jett, knowing he never expected this. This would radically change everything. His life in Los Angeles would be over. "Oh, God, Jett. I'm so sorry," I whispered in his ear. "We'll figure this out."

"Fuck, Asia. How'd things get this out of hand?" He held me tightly.

"I'm not sure. For now, act happy."

"Yeah, you're right." We let each other go, and he waved at his parents. "I'll do my best. Thank you."

His mom and dad came off the stage and right to us, hugging us both. His mother held me out and looked at me with tears in her green eyes. "We didn't want miles to come between you two every week. Now, you'll see your husband every night, the way a marriage should be. Los Angeles is a thing of the past for Jett. His future is here on the East Coast with you and one day, your children."

I smiled even though inside I was crying for Jett. He had no idea our fake marriage would cost him so much. His carefree days away from it all in Los Angeles seemed to be behind him. Now he had the responsibility of making sure the whole company ran smoothly.

He and I had never talked about his job. I had no idea if he wanted that kind of responsibility yet or not. But I was pretty sure, he didn't want that. Not at that moment in time.

The band started playing, and Jett took me in his arms. It was then that I felt him shaking. I felt so badly for him. He never knew this would be thrust upon him. I knew it then, he was in over his head.

"I think you'll make a great CEO, Jett."

He looked at me with a frown on his handsome face. "Do you think that was a thing I wanted? Because it's not. I never meant for this thing to change my entire life, Asia. I've made a mistake."

My heart ached for him, but also for me. He looked like a tiger who'd just been caged, and he would do anything to get out of that cage and get back to the freedom of the wild.

I didn't know what to say to the man. Lies are the root of all evil, right there next to money. If we could've gone back in time, I'd have cautioned him about what might happen. I had no idea his parents would give him the CEO job just because he said he was married, and I knew Jett didn't think that, either.

After the song was over, Jett took me by the hand and led me away to a remote corner of the large room. He and I took seats and were quickly served Champagne. He gulped his tall glass down, then I handed him mine. "Here, you need this more than I do."

"Thank you." He took it from me and gulped it down too. "What's happened, Asia? How did things get so completely out of my control?"

"I'm not sure. I think you should talk to your parents tomorrow and explain that you're not ready for this."

Sebastien Greenberg and his older sister, Madison approached us. Sebastien held out his hand to me. "A dance with the bride, please."

I looked at Jett who nodded. "It's tradition for the bride and groom to dance with whoever asks them."

I feigned graciousness. "Of course, Sebastien." I didn't want to dance with him. I didn't want to leave Jett's side, but I had to. Fucking social etiquette dictated that!

And as soon as I was led away by her brother, Madison swooped in on Jett like a hawk on her prey. He got up and took her long, bony-ass hand and followed us out onto the dance floor.

I couldn't take my eyes off them. I was a jealous mess. Jett's hand rested on the small of her back, their other hands clasped. He did leave space between them, but as the song went on, the bitch managed to move in a bit at a time until their bodies were flush against each other's

Sebastien pulled me close. "You're a great dancer, Asia."

"Jett taught me. That's why I'm any good at all."

"Oh, I bet you were always good. I doubt he'd take all the credit for you." He spun me around, and we ended up next to Jett and Madison who were talking in whispers to one another.

It was like torture, watching them!

"I bet he'd take all the credit. He's taught me everything."

Turning me the other direction, Sebastien took me away from them just as the song ended. "How about another dance, Asia?"

Jett looked around the room then his eyes landed on me. He smiled and let Madison's hand go as he came towards me. "No thank you, Sebastien."

I met Jett in the middle of the room. "I hated that." He pulled me into his arms. "I don't give a flying fuck about tradition. I'm changing that shit with us. My wife dances only with me."

A deep sigh came out of me. "And my husband only dances with me."

We danced the rest of the night away, just like the story we made up about the first night we met. Things were moving along, maybe not how we expected them to, but like all things, what we had was moving forward.

Maybe the pace was too fast, but it seemed we were helpless to slow it down.

# 25

# JETT

It was our last night at my parent's vacation home. The party was over, and so was the first reason for having a fake wife. Things had happened that shouldn't have.

I was given the role of CEO. That meant I had to stay in New York. My beach house in Malibu would become only a vacation home. My life, as I had known it, was over.

Along the way, I'd fallen in love with my sub. A thing that was stupid on my part.

Asia was young, beautiful, and had a bright future ahead of her. And she was as naive as they come. The next morning we were saying our goodbyes and heading back to Harrison. There were three more functions I needed her for, then we'd see what would happen between us.

My mother had tears in her eyes when we drove away. She made us promise to call her as soon as Asia's parents could make it to a dinner party. She was dying to meet them.

I was dying to end the lies with them. But I didn't know how to. I had until the end of August to continue my vacation. On September 1st, I was supposed to report to our headquarters in New York City to begin the transfer of power over the company from my father to me.

Was I ready for that?

No, fucking way!

But I had yet to figure out exactly how to get out of it. About the only thing I'd come up with was if Asia and I broke up. Then I could say I was too shattered to deal with that responsibility.

If I stayed with Asia, it meant I'd have to take over from Dad. Was I ready for any of that?

I didn't think so.

"Would you put the top down, Jett?" Asia ran her fingertips over my cheek. "Fresh air would be nice."

Pulling to the side of the road, I dropped the top then started going again. "My mother told me she's changed her mind about us waiting to have kids. She thinks we have something real and extraordinary. She'd like to see grandchildren by Christmas next year."

Asia laughed and threw her hands into the air, letting the wind rush past them. "Oh, the craziness of life, Jett!" She turned her pretty face and leaned her head on the headrest. "We could just actually go to Vegas, get married for real, and do just that, Jett."

Glancing at her, I thought she had to be joking. But her expression was serious. "Asia, marriage is a serious thing to me."

She sighed and turned her head to look up at the afternoon sky. "I know. I was just saying, it could be done. Then we'd never have to tell your family how we lied to them. They're very nice people, Jett. They treated me like family. It was so, so… wonderful." She looked away from me.

I ran my hand over her shoulder. "People shouldn't actually get married just to cover up their lies."

"You're right." She looked at me again. "Can I be honest?"

"Yes." I put both hands on the wheel as I tried to brace myself for her honesty. I wasn't sure what she was about to say but knew I was probably going to have an issue with it.

"I never expected to like them. I thought they'd be typical rich snooty people. But they weren't. They were down to earth, and I really grew to care about them all. Even the pesky twins, Jett. If this ends, what we have, it'll leave a hole the size of the Grand Canyon in my heart and soul."

And there it was!

I would hurt her immensely if I ended things.

"Wow, no pressure there, Asia," my tone was sharp. I hadn't meant it to be. But there it was, sharp and a bit on the bitter side.

She looked away without saying another word. As a matter of fact, she didn't say a thing for the rest of the ride home. Silence is golden some say. That period of silence was anything but golden, it was more black and dark, ominous and deep as an abyss.

When we parked in the garage at home, Asia got out of the car. She walked inside as I sat in the car and gripped the steering wheel as I tried not to scream.

I felt like I was on a see-saw. Up one minute, down the next. I loved Asia, I knew I did. But was my love for her going to last? And if it did, would it be enough to stop me from going back to being the selfish man I'd always been?

I wasn't sure. And I never knew if I'd become sure.

The lie of a marriage was turning on me, like a pet dragon that began to yearn for its' freedom. It was breathing its' fire on me, trying its' best to make me let it go.

We had a wedding to go to in one week. Greg Blankenship, my college roommate, a man my exact age, was about to make Sandra Goldenbloom his lawfully wedded wife. In front of their families and friends, they were going to make it real.

And I was going to take my fake wife to see them step into a real marriage. It all seemed very pathetic then.

Getting out of the car, I went inside. Straight to the kitchen, I went, getting myself a beer then going to sit in the den to drink alone. One beer turned into ten as I sat there, staring out the window at the beautifully manicured lawn. When the sun set, the lights came on, filling the dark corners so intruders wouldn't feel safe in our yard.

I hadn't bothered to turn the lights on in the room. Darkness seemed more fitting for how I was feeling.

In a chair that faced a window, I sat perfectly still. Soft hands ran around from behind me, a light breath warmed my ear. "You should come to bed."

Running my hand up her arm, I mumbled, "You don't hate me?"

"I could never hate you. Come to bed. Tomorrow will be another day. Things always have a way of looking brighter in the sun's light." She slipped around the side of the chair and gently sat on my lap.

Her dark hair was hanging in damp strands. I ran my hand through them. "Asia, I'm not who I seem to be. I'm a very selfish man. I'd make a shitty real husband. Can you understand that? You deserve a great husband. I can't be that for you."

"Jett, you and I have a contract. I'm to be whatever you want me to be until August 31st. If you want a sub, I will be that. If you want a fake wife, I will be that. I will be whatever you want me to. Leave the real things out of it for now."

My throat was growing tight, tears were filling my eyes as I looked at the most beautiful and understanding woman in the entire world. "I love you, Asia."

Her smile tugged at my heart. "And I love you, Jett. Now come to bed and let's get some sleep. We've had a long, hard week. We need to rest up for the coming weekend, and all that will entail. Let's spend this week chilling by our pool, maybe taking in a movie, and doing some normal things. What do you say to that?"

"I say, that sounds great, baby. Especially the part where you told me that you love me. You mean that, right?"

She nodded, got off my lap, and took me by the hand. "I love you, Jett Simmons. No matter what the future holds for us, for now just know that I love you, for real."

She led me up the stairs all the way to our bedroom. A room I'd found I missed when she took me through the door. It smelled like she and I mixed all up together. It smelled like home.

Could I really make a home with her? Would she want to put up with me and my ways forever?

There was a lot of doubt in my mind that she would want to put up with me.

I sat on the edge of the bed, at her prompting and she undressed me, then helped me get underneath the covers. She pulled her robe off, and laid next to me, naked in our bed.

Asia pulled my arm out, and laid her head on my shoulder then pulled my arm to wrap around her. It was the way we'd slept together since the very first night. "I never want us to go to bed angry, okay?"

"Okay, baby." I turned my head, and she kissed me, sweetly. "Goodnight, my love."

"Goodnight, Jett. I love you. Now, have some sweet dreams."

With a sigh, I closed my eyes and let myself fall away from it all and sank into a deep sleep.

## 26

## ASIA

It was the night before the wedding. Jett and I had gotten along great the whole week. We did normal things as we hung out together and life was easy.

That night, when we went to bed, things got odd.

"We have to be ready to go by noon. The driver will be here, and he'll take us to New York. This time around, I want you to be quiet as a church mouse. I don't want anyone getting too close to you. I don't want Greg and Sandra to think we'll be going and doing a bunch of things together as married couples. Got it?" He pulled off his shorts and climbed into bed.

"Okay, get to know no one. I understand, completely. We won't have a rerun of what happened with your family, Jett. I promise." I pulled off my clothes and climbed into bed too.

We usually made love before we went to sleep, but Jett turned over and turned out his lamp and stayed turned over. I was lying on my back, staring at the ceiling.

Why the sudden onset of worry? Why was he shutting me out?

Jett was a complex man. His parents didn't seem to notice it, but I did. He was immature in a lot of ways. I guess not ever being serious with a woman had him bouncing back and forth along the relationship spectrum.

One day, he'd be all about us. The next, it was how he was going to do this, and he was going to do that.

I'd never had a relationship to compare it to, but I knew he was yo-yoing about making things real with me. Even though I made sure not to say a word about wanting anything past August 31st.

That night I slept terribly, and the next morning Jett rushed me, making me anxious and nervous. He was so cool towards me. The entire ride there, he was on his cell. Doing what, I didn't know. All I knew was he was distractingg himself. Trying to stay away from me. Then we arrived at the chapel, and he ran his arm around me and turned into the man he normally was with me. There was a man in a blue suit who met us at the door. "Jett Simmons, you old dog." He grabbed Jett's hand and shook it. "Long time, no see."

"Jason, this is my wife, Asia." Jett looked at me as I shook his old friend's hand. "We hung out together in college." He turned his attention back to Jason. "How's Greg? A mess I bet."

"Nah, he's cool." Jason smiled at me. "Sandra's a great girl, he knows that and has been ready to change her last name for a while now. She made him wait a whole year. Not like what I hear about you two." He gently punched Jett in the arm. "You two met and married in no time, is the word on the street. You'll have to give me the rundown at the reception."

"How'd you hear about us?" Jett asked as he looked curiously at his friend.

"The Greenberg's are here. Sebastien and Madison. Madison was Sandra's college roommate, and she's her maid of honor." Jason winked at me. "Sebastien told me you were gorgeous. How right he was. But we all knew Jett wouldn't settle for just any old girl."

Jett gave me a sideways glance. "Sebastien said that, did he. Seems you made quite an impression on the kid, baby. We should go find a place to sit. See you, Jason."

Jett moved his arm down my back and took my hand. "Was I quiet enough or too quiet?"

"You did fine. Funny that neither of them mentioned they were attending a wedding, isn't it?" We walked into the church, and Jett looked around the already crowded church. Also looking around was Sebastien. He waved at us and pointed to the empty space next to him. "Well, would you look at that. Seems your boyfriend saved you a seat. How sweet of him."

"You sound jealous, Jett." I followed behind him as he looked as if he was heading right to the man who was provoking said jealousy.

Jett stopped two rows behind Sebastien who was all smiles as he looked at me. He tugged me along behind him past a group of older women, and we sat at the far end of the row. Sebastien turned around with a frown on his face. "Little shit," Jett growled. "No dancing at the reception unless it's with me."

"Ten-four." I looked down and smoothed out my pink dress. Jett wore a black suit and looked extraordinarily hot. I wrapped my arm around his. "I love weddings."

"Humph!" That was all I got out of him.

Music began, and three little girls came down the aisle, tossing daisies along the way. "Aren't they precious?"

Jett didn't make a sound in response. He wasn't even looking, I found out when I turned to see what he was doing. Jett was looking at the windows. They were stained glass and gorgeous, but I didn't think they were so spectacular that he'd look at them, instead of at what was going on.

His body was tense, and he'd become very uncomfortable. I reached out and took his hand and found it clammy. Leaning in, I whispered, "Are you feeling well?"

He turned to look at me with a grim face then whispered back, "I'm kind of sick to my stomach. I've never felt more pathetic in my entire life, thanks to this sham of a marriage."

There was nothing I could say to him that would make him feel better at that moment. The only words running through my head were, 'maybe you should've thought things through before you went to so far as to purchase a sub to make her your fake wife.' But that would've only made him feel worse.

The music changed, and I focused on the wedding, instead of the brooding man who sat next to me. The bridesmaids and groomsmen filed down the aisle. The pretty girls wore yellow chiffon, and the men all wore black tuxedos. Madison came down the aisle last and alone. She was dressed in a different dress. Hers was off-white and much nicer than the rest of the girls.

Her eyes roamed, and she gave a nod our way, though her eyes looked past me. Out of the corner of my eye, I saw Jett had turned his attention back to the wedding, and he gave Madison a nod back.

I bit my lower lip and tried to keep my mouth shut. I don't know exactly what it was about the two of them that made me see red. But I hated how she was clearly after Jett. Even though she thought he was a married man.

The woman was a homewrecker, waiting to happen. Maybe a nice dose of laxative in her drink at the reception would be in order for the tramp. I made a mental note to ask our driver to stop off at a drug store. I'd say I needed some aspirin for a headache and get that instead. At the very least, it'd keep the bitch out of my hair for the night.

The music changed once more, the bridal march came on, and we all stood for the entrance of the bride. Covered in white with a veil that hid her face, Sandra, a woman I'd never met, walked slowly down the aisle.

Strong hands ran around my waist as Jett pulled me back against his chest. His lips touched my ear. "You deserve something like this, baby."

I ran my hand up to caress his cheek and sighed. There he was, back to the romantic man he was most of the time with me. His lips pressed against the top of my head, sending sparks all through me.

When she made it to her groom, we all sat back down. Jett took my hand and held it tightly. We watched the couple take their vows then Jett looked at me as the couple kissed. I smiled then mouthed, 'I love you.'

He leaned in and gave me a kiss. "I love you, too."

Maybe the night at the reception wouldn't be as bad as I thought it was going to be with him in a foul mood. Maybe the wedding was putting good ideas into Jett's head.

With the bride and groom running down the aisle, we all stood up and clapped. Jett held me tight and kissed the side of my neck. "I want you, Asia. In the car."

Turning my head, I wasn't sure what he meant. I didn't say a word, though. My body heated as I thought about he and I in the back of the limo, getting a bit beastly.

We moved with the crowd out of the church. The newly wedded couple had already gotten into a car and were heading to the hotel where the reception would soon be held.

Jett and I headed to the car as the driver waited at the back door. I got in, followed by Jett. He pushed the button that raised the dark privacy window that separated us from the driver. I shivered with desire.

The seat was long and ran along the back of the limo. The floor was open. "On your knees," he ordered me before we'd even begun to take off.

With delight, I did as he'd said to, getting on my knees as he pushed my dress up and slid my panties down. I was already wet for him with the idea. The windows were darkly tinted and I knew no one could see in, but I could see people as they walked around the car.

My heart was pounding as he moved in behind me, thrusting his hard cock into me. He grunted with each hard thrust. I balled my fists up and moved back to meet each thrust. It felt dirty and I loved it!

My attention was taken as Madison and Sebastien came right toward the car. I held my breath as I watched them approach it. "Jett, are they coming with us? Or what?"

He looked up to find Madison reaching for the door handle, and quickly locked the doors. "What the fuck is she thinking?"

She knocked on the window. "Jett, are you in there?"

"What the hell does she want?" I asked as anger filled me.

"Fuck if I know. Shit!" He pulled out of me as I scrambled to pull my panties up. Huffing and puffing, I sat on the seat and made sure my dress was smoothed out.

Jett rolled the window down only a bit. "Can I help you, Madison?"

"Sebastien and I need a ride. Seems we missed ours. Do you mind, terribly if we go to the reception with you two?"

He cut his eyes at me, and I saw raw anger in them. Then he unlocked the door and took my hand, pulling me to the seat across from the one we were seated on.

They got in, both smiling away. "Thanks, man." Sebastien nodded at Jett then looked at me. "Well, don't you look as pretty as a picture. Save a dance for me, Asia."

My stomach knotted as Jett squeezed my hand. "Oh, she will. Madison, you save one for me too."

"For sure!" She nearly bounced off the fucking seat with joy.

I reached behind me to knock on the window, and our driver put it down. "Yes?"

"Can we make a quick stop at a drug store on the way, please. I have an awful headache, and need to run in to buy something to get rid of it?"

"Sure thing, Mrs. Simmons." He rolled the window back up, and I smiled like nothing was bothering me at all.

There was something bothering me. But soon she'd be stuck in the bathroom. Her big-ass dress, making things even harder for her. Poor Madison Greenberg was about to find out what happens when you keep stepping on my toes!

## 27

# JETT

The reception wasn't the place I wanted to be. Something about that wedding was working on me like a burr under a saddle. Guilt, remorse, anger, and even a tad bit of self-loathing was combining inside of me, creating a shit-storm.

Asia looked like a doll in a dark blue dress and matching heels. The neckline was scooped on the knee length dress that was reminiscent of the style women wore in the fifties. She wore a strand of pearls that hugged her neck, almost like a choker. Her dark, silky hair was curled, loosely. Everyone noticed her, even though she was going for a demure look.

That woman had no idea of how beautiful she truly was. The beauty went all the way through her. She wore a sweet smile as she went to get us some of the wedding cake that was cut after the meal of roasted chicken was over.

I watched Asia as she went behind the elaborate wedding cake to pick up pieces that had already been sliced. She emerged from the other side with three plates. Cocking my head to one side, I wondered why she had three pieces of cake. Then I watched her make her way to the table where the newly married couple and their wedding party were seated.

Amazingly enough, she went to Madison and gave her one of the pieces. The two exchanged smiles and I could see Madison was thanking her. Then Asia came to me. We'd been seated at a table with six people I didn't know.

That's one of the reasons I hated to go alone to weddings. Whoever was in charge of the seating arrangements always seemed to love to make people who didn't know one another sit together. It was a vain attempt at widening one's circle of friends, I suppose. Whatever the reason, I hated it. I hated making small talk and when you're sitting with a bunch of strangers it's impossible to do anything else.

Asia took her seat next to me and stabbed my pieces of cake with the little plastic fork it was served with. She held the bite to my lips and I took it as I looked at her. Then I took her fork and did the same to her. Seemed we were going to feed each other.

"Pretty good." She picked up the fresh glass of Champagne that had been served to us all after she left the table to go after the cake.

"I noticed you took a piece to Madison." I gave her another bite. "Are you thinking of trying to become her friend or something?"

"Oh, I don't know about that." She fed me another piece of the dry chocolate cake. That was another thing about weddings that I hated. The cake's always dry.

Did they make the things a month in advance or what?

"No more for me, thanks." I pushed my plate away and picked up my glass.

Asia grinned and leaned in to whisper, "It's pretty terrible."

"Dry as the Sahara."

She pushed her plate away too and smiled at me. "The band will start playing soon. They're getting on stage now. You really don't expect me to dance with Sebastien and you with Madison, do you?"

"I was feeling prickly in the car. I don't know what made me say that. I'm feeling prickly now too. I'm not sure why that is, but that's how I'm feeling." I leaned back in my chair and draped my arm around the back of hers.

She leaned back and looked at me. "Would you like to leave? Our room is just upstairs."

We'd gotten a room in the hotel to stay in for the night, instead of going back home. And I did want to leave, but I knew that would be rude. "We have to stay, Asia."

She nodded and looked around the large room that was decorated in golden hues. "Everything is so pretty. I wonder how long it took to plan this whole thing out."

"A year," came a woman's reply.

Asia looked at the woman who was seated at our table. "Goodness, that's a long time."

The older woman with blue tint to her black hair nodded. "It is. But that's about the time frame most weddings take to plan. Did you two not have a traditional wedding?"

"We got married in Vegas." Asia put her hand on my leg as she told the lie. "We just couldn't wait. Isn't that right, honey?"

"Yeah." I wasn't in a chatty mood.

The fact was, the lie was beginning to get stuck in my craw, whatever a craw is. It felt like it might be somewhere between my heart and my soul. Asia seemed to be just fine with it, though. She kept on chatting away with the woman she didn't know and shouldn't have been wasting her time on, "We met in a night club in Los Angeles."

"You did?" The woman rested her chin on her entwined fingers. "I met my husband on a cruise to Alaska. He and I met at one of the buffets and ended up sitting together. We just kept meeting up the whole week and then started dating once the cruise was over. I lived in the Midwest and he lived on the east coast. It was a long dating period. Two whole years. Then I moved to be with him and he asked me to marry him after we'd lived together for a year. It took a year to plan our wedding. It was so beautiful. Do you ever regret the fact you missed out on that?"

Asia shook her head. "Not one bit." She patted my leg. "I love how fast everything happened for us. It was like it was meant to be and there was no stopping the train that was our love as it sped down the tracks."

I rolled my eyes as someone on stage began to talk. It silenced the chatting that was annoying me. The lie felt like it was getting bigger, growing into a beast that would eventually kill us both.

The first song was played and the bride and groom danced as we all watched. Then the next song came on and others joined them on the dance floor. My eyes caught Sebastien as he walked up behind Asia.

"May I have this dance?"

Asia looked at me for that answer. For reasons I can't explain, it pissed me off. Why didn't she just tell him no, on her own? Why was she looking at me as if asking if she could dance with the little shit?

And why did I growl, "Go dance with the man, Asia."

Her brow furrowed. "Are you sure?"

Sebastien ran his hand over her shoulder, down her arm and took her hand in his. The hand that had my rings on it. The hand that belonged to me. "He'll be fine. Madison is on her way to take him to the dance floor."

I looked up to find Madison walking towards me and then looked at Asia. "Yeah, just go, Asia." My jaw was clenched. My body tense. Asia could make up her own mind about things. Yet, she was acting as if she needed me to tell her not to dance with the little prick. And as hard as I was looking at her to get her to understand that, she wasn't getting it.

She got up and went with him and I was left, sitting alone. Madison came up to me with a smile curving her thin red lips. "Fancy a twirl on the dance floor, Jett?"

I got up, grabbed her by the hand and took off to the dance floor. Moving in right behind Asia and Sebastien, I overheard him as he leaned in close and whispered, "My God, you look gorgeous tonight."

"Thank you," came Asia's reply.

"I'm going to be a bother to your husband tonight. Stealing you away is all I can think about." His words hit me like a brick.

I don't recall how it all happened. Pure anger sped through me, took me over and all I knew was that I was looking at Sebastien Greenberg as he was laid out on the dance floor. His eyes were closed and a red bump on his chin was getting redder by the second.

"Jett!" Madison shouted then doubled over and held her stomach.

"What the?" She turned and ran off and I saw Asia grinning like the Cheshire cat from Alice in Wonderland as she watched her run.

I reached over Sebastien's fallen body, took Asia by the hand and left the room. "Should I even ask for an explanation, Jett?"

"No."

Without saying a word, I took her up to our hotel room, closed the door and leaned back on it. My head was spinning. I wasn't sure about anything. I'd never been so rash. I'd never done anything like that.

What was happening to me?

# 28

# ASIA

Jett was over the top. I was sure he'd overheard what Sebastien had said to me about stealing me away. But punching the guy out was uncalled for.

As much as I didn't agree with his actions, I had to admit, I was impressed. And I'd done something just as bad myself. The cake I took to Madison had a nice size bite of what seemed to be a chunk of chocolate, but was really a chunk of fast-acting laxative. And it seemed to hit her at just about the same time Jett hit her brother.

In our hotel room, I stood and watched Jett as he leaned against the door and looked at the floor. "This isn't working for me, Asia."

Everything in me stopped; my heart, my lungs, my life. I didn't know what to say. I found myself staggering back until my legs hit the bed, then I sat on it and tried hard not to pass out.

It was over. He didn't want me anymore.

All I could do was shake my head and try not to cry. I had no idea what I'd done wrong. I didn't know what I could do to make things right. "I'll leave."

"What?" He came to me and got on his knees in front of me, taking my hands. "Why?"

My eyes were clouding with tears. "Because of what you said. This isn't working for you." A sob came out of me, and I sucked it back in as best I could.

I was his sub. I wasn't supposed to make him feel guilty for anything he did. He didn't want me, that was his right.

"I didn't mean that. I meant the lie." He took my chin in his hand and rubbed the pad of his thumb across my lips. "You deserve a real love. You deserve so much more than I'm giving you. Making you lie about a marriage feels wrong to me now."

I didn't understand at all. "Why would you be okay with lying to your family? But lying to a bunch of strangers bothers you?"

"I can't explain it. The wedding just brought things to my mind. Things like you deserving to have a real wedding. You deserving to have a truthful relationship. I took that all away from you, Asia."

"Look, things aren't that bad, Jett. I signed the contract. I knew what I was doing. And I feel lucky that you got me. I could be strung up in some dungeon right now, being whipped into submission. Instead, I'm in a fancy hotel with a man who cares a hell of a lot about me. Things could be worse."

He looked at me with storm clouds in his sea green eyes. "Asia, you're too good to be true. I don't know how you do it. You can take my foul mood and turn it all around. Maybe it's hearing you lie that upsets me so much. I don't like that it's me who made you do that. I don't like that it's me who's making you into a liar."

"Do you feel like I'm a liar, Jett?" The thought irritated me.

He nodded. "You're all into the act of being my wife. It's as if you're actually believing the shit that's coming out of your mouth. The whole front story. The way you touch me. It all seems so true when you tell it or touch me. You're a little too good at it. Like it was in you the whole time." He moved his hand off my face and got up, turning his back to me. "Have I turned you into a liar?"

I didn't know what the hell to say to that. He paid me to be his fake wife and make people believe his whole story. And I was doing as he wanted me to. "It was you who didn't think things through, Jett. Don't blame me for going along with you and saying things you told me to say."

He spun around with a glare. "Asia, the number one thing I told you was to be quiet. Don't say anything unless I ask you to. And there you went on a trip down a false memory lane with a fucking stranger. That woman didn't need to know a thing about us. She's nobody to me."

"Okay, I admit, I forgot about being quiet. Fuck, Jett!"

Getting up, I kicked off my shoes and went to the mini fridge to see what kind of alcohol was in it. My brain was pulsing with aggravation. If Jett told me to go left, I went left. If he told me to jump, I jumped. But now the problem was not that I was doing as he'd told me to, but that I was doing it for too damn long.

I was sick of it.

"And why in the hell did you look at me for an answer when that dumb-fuck asked you to dance? Are you without a will of your own, Asia?" His hand was on my shoulder, spinning me back around just as I'd reached the fridge.

"You have me confused, Jett. That's why I looked at you for the answer. You told him in the car that he could dance with me. You told me later not to dance with him. And when he asked me, I thought you'd be the one to tell him no. I didn't know what to do then you told me to go dance with him and I did."

"And he told you he wanted to steal you away from me. And you did nothing." His glare penetrated me, it was so intense.

"You hit him before I could say a word."

"What would you have said to him?"

I shook my head. "I don't know. I didn't exactly have a chance to think about it. You'd spun him around so quickly, it nearly made me fall. I was concentrating on staying on my feet. And then you punched him, and I was shocked. I don't know what I would've said. But I probably would've told him that was inappropriate and probably walked off the dance floor."

"I've never been that mad." He turned away from me. "Frankly, I don't like it."

Turning back to the fridge, I found small bottles of all kinds of things and pulled out a bottle of vodka. I needed something that would take the edge off and quick.

The man was making me nuts.

"Sorry for making you give a shit about me, Jett."

"Jealousy isn't comfortable, Asia. And what are you doing?" He held out his hand, wanting me to surrender the tiny bottle I was chugging on, to him. "Are my actions not only turning you into a liar but an alcoholic too? I'm very bad for you."

Maybe he was right. Maybe he was bad for me.

Sure, my life with him was full of lavish things, and the lifestyle itself was grandiose. But he was right. I was falling into lying quite easily. And turning to alcohol to still my nerves had never been a thing I'd done before knowing him.

Maybe it was all too good to be true.

Maybe we were both trying too damn hard to make a relationship when neither of us was looking for one.

The lie of a marriage seemed to be too much pressure to put on two people who hadn't even had normal relationships in the past. "We should stop this, Jett. We should go to a normal Dom/sub relationship. Only do the pretend marriage when we have to. We're living as if we're married. Sharing the same bed, doing things as a couple, instead of what we really are to one another. You are my owner. For the matter of one more month anyway. This is just too much pressure on us both."

I handed him the half empty bottle. He put it down and took me in his strong arms, rocking me back and forth then kissed the top of my head. "I'm more than just your owner, baby. You know that. And I think the fake marriage is undue stress. You have no idea how guilty I feel about it now. But I don't want a normal Dom/sub relationship with you. You're my girlfriend. Not my wife, not my submissive partner. You're my very first real girlfriend. And I'm your first boyfriend. The lie is robbing us of what would be a normal thing. And it's all my fault. I wanted to take what I perceived as the easy way out of situations that I felt would be uncomfortable. For the sake of bypassing that feeling, I made an innocent girl lie and miss out on having a nice, normal relationship. For that I am sorry. But I'm not sorry that I found you and made you mine. I'll never be sorry about that."

What he said made sense to me. We'd passed up normal right from the start though. How does one go back to a place they've never been before?

## 29

# JETT

I didn't know how I was going to change things, but I was slowly growing more determined to make some drastic changes. Swaying with Asia in my arms, my heart grew soft, and I wanted to show her she meant more to me than anyone ever had.

Turning her around, I unhooked the necklace then unzipped her dress. "How about we get into bed?"

It wasn't but five in the evening, but I was tired. Tired in so many ways. Who knew that making up a false marriage could be so damn tiring?

As I pushed the dress down, exposing her creamy shoulder, I ran my lips over it. "I love you, Asia." My heart was swelling with that love. I hated the intense reactions I had over her, but I fucking loved that woman. I'd kill for her, or at least wound a man, it seemed. Caring for someone that way, was new to me. And not comfortable in the least.

Her hands caught up in my hair as she whispered, "I love you, Jett." She moved her hands under my jacket, taking it off me. It fell to the floor, joining her dress.

Moving my hands over her shoulders to her back, her skin felt like silk. Her body felt good in my arms. I lifted her up and took her to the bed, laying her on it and looking at her. I didn't deserve her, but I wasn't going to let her go.

Trailing one finger down her stomach, I slid my fingers into the top of her blue satin panties and pulled them off her. Her bra was all that was left, and I took it away too. Her body was naked and gorgeous. My cock was rising in need to feel her. I finished undressing myself then laid on my side next to her, leaning up on my hand and stroking her stomach.

The wedding ring on my finger glistened, and I thought about what I should do about the thing. I took it off then took the rings off her finger too. We'd be what we really were. Not the fake married couple I felt was ruining what we really had found.

The smile she gave me told me she got what I was doing. She ran her hands up and down my chest. "Hi, I'm Asia and single."

"Hi, I'm Jett, and looking."

"Are you?" She ran her hands up, taking my face between them. "What is it you're looking for?"

"A women with a gorgeous body, stunning face, beautiful heart, and it wouldn't hurt if she were a real tiger in bed. Do you happen to know anyone like that?"

Her cheeks went pink as she batted at my chest. "You sweet talker."

"I only speak the truth, my little Asia." I leaned over, taking her plump, rosebud lips with mine, leaving them with a nibble then looking down at her once more.

I really could look at her forever, it seemed. Her eyes were closed, then she opened them. "You know, now that I think about it, I'm looking too. You don't happen to know where I could find a strong, handsome, sweet, caring, virile man who knows his way around a woman's body, do you?"

"I might." I caressed her breast as I gazed into her brown eyes. "If I find one, what should I tell him you want with him?"

"You can tell him that I'm looking for a man I can have fun with, talk to like we're old friends, do silly things with, and find a love to end all loves with." She put her hand over mine and pulled it down to her sweet spot. "And learn new and exciting ways to please each other, sexually."

"Oh, baby. I know a guy who'd be so right for you. Now, he's a bit on the brooding selfish side, I hope you can take him with all his flaws and faults. He can be foolish, stubborn, pig-headed-"

She stopped me with a kiss as she pulled her head up off the pillow. "And wonderful too. Mostly, he's wonderful."

"You think?" I grinned at her as I moved my hand in a way that would please her. Her clit pulsed under my fingertip.

She nodded. "I do."

Asia was something else. A woman who could take my heart and run away with it. And I was beginning to let her do just that. Giving into her was easy. The hard part was learning where to draw the lines we both needed.

As I kissed her, I moved my body over hers and pressed my cock into her warm recesses. She pulled her legs up, bending her knees. Her hands roamed over my back as we both moaned. There was nowhere better to be than inside of her.

My lips left hers to nuzzle her neck and kiss the soft place behind her ear. Our bodies moved in slow waves, taking us out of our heads to a place we were fast becoming familiar with. A place only she and I could go.

Heat radiated off her and I as we began to move faster, the urgency to get to the release taking us over. The beast inside me grew. The soft kissing wasn't enough anymore. I bit her between the shoulder and neck as I took her hands and held them down over her head.

She moaned and arched up to me as I pulled back to watch her give me what I wanted. "I want you to give it to me, Asia. Give it all to me."

Her body was quivering as she looked at me. "Together, Jett. Let's do this together. I'll hold back until you're ready."

And I knew then exactly what she meant. She'd hold back until I was emotionally ready to be more than what we were then. She'd wait, patiently for me to grow the way I needed to. How long would that take, I didn't know, but I had the sense that she'd wait for however long it took me to become the man she deserved.

Thrusting into her soft body, I was acutely aware of how fragile she was and how powerful I was. I had the power to break her, but she had the same power I did.

She could so easily break me.

It would be so easy, it scared me.

But as I looked into her eyes, eyes that held strength I'm sure she had no idea she possessed, I saw the love she had for me. She wouldn't break me. If she did, she'd hurt herself too.

I was safe with her. There was no need for fear. With her, I'd always be safe. And she'd be safe with me. I was about to make sure of that.

My inner demons that sought to put doubt in my mind grew silent as I plunged into her, taking her strength and giving her mine. We needed to share our strengths. I wasn't her master, her owner. She and I were equals, with different attributes. Just like a great business, two minds were better than one.

There I was, thrusting away, trying my hardest to get to where she was. I wanted to be there with her. I wanted that peace of mind. That serenity of soul, she'd gotten to before me.

And just as that thought went through my head, she did something inside of her that gripped my cock and took me over the edge. She came too, and we both made loud war cries as our bodies converged into something that almost seemed unreal.

I fell on top of her, barely able to breathe. We both shook as the orgasms quaked within us. I could feel hers, and she could feel mine. I'd never shared sex so deeply before. Not ever.

It felt as if our souls connected then. The falseness that had brought us together was gone. She wasn't a woman I had a contract with. She wasn't my sub or fake wife. But she was mine, and I was hers.

In that moment, in that time, we were just us. A couple of people who were finding out that we had a lot within us that connected. I found a new part of me, and I thought she might've found something new in her too.

Once I'd caught my breath, I pulled my head up, my hair damp as it clung to my face. "Hi, I'm Jett Simmons. It's nice to make your acquaintance."

"Hi there, Jett Simmons. I'm Asia Jones. I think we should date. What do you think?"

"I think that's a great idea. I'd love nothing more than to call you my girlfriend."

"K." She laughed, lightly. "Boyfriend."

Kissing her again, our deal was sealed. We were normal. A nice normal couple. Not a couple of liars. Not a couple of people in an odd contract. Just a couple. A nice normal couple.

## 30

## ASIA

We spooned as we slept the rest of the evening away at the hotel. All the way through until the next morning, we slept. When I opened my eyes, I saw the three rings that were on the nightstand next to me. The weight of the heavy rings was off me. And I very much liked it. Part of me wondered if that was wrong of me. I loved Jett after all. Wearing his ring, even if under false pretenses, should feel great, right?

But the way it felt with them off was obvious. It couldn't be ignored. The feeling was great. I felt light, airy, and normal.

Jett's arm was flung over me, and so was one leg. It was the usual way I'd woken up since the first night we were together. Nothing was different, yet it felt different.

His body jerked then he rolled over and stretched as he yawned loudly. "Damn, we slept all night long."

"We must've been very tired." I turned over to lay on my other side so I could see him.

"I think you're right." He rolled over to face me and kissed the tip of my nose. "Hey, girlfriend."

"Hey, boyfriend." I laughed and threw my arm over him then kissed his cheek.

"Aren't we just too cute?" he asked then rolled over and got out of bed. "Let's get showered, dressed then I'm calling the car to come take us home. I don't want to see anyone who'll fuck up our day."

"I'm with you. You shower then I will."

He stopped walking away and turned to look at me. "Why?"

"Well, I don't think newly dating couples shower together." I winked at him.

"Get your ass up and come get in the shower with me. We're not going back to square one. We're just not acting married."

I laughed as I got up and followed him to the bathroom. It had been almost two months that we'd been acting married. We had no bathroom rules, we did as married people did. We'd put privacy away and had immersed ourselves in that lifestyle.

It had been hard for me in the beginning, but I started liking it. Being with Jett was easy. He made it that way.

We brushed our teeth in the double sinks, took turns peeing, then got into the small shower. It was a normal sized shower, not like the one in our house.

As I thought about that, it made a bit of the weight I'd been carrying show itself. He and I did share a home. We were closer to being married than not being married. Even if it had all begun with a lie.

His hands ran through my hair as he shampooed it while I ran my soapy hands all over his upper body. We'd really gotten into a routine. I washed his back, he washed mine. We didn't even have to talk, we just did like we always had.

"How did this happen, Jett?" I asked as if he could read my mind. But somehow he had. "I'm not sure. The faking turned real at some time that neither of us seemed to notice."

I began to wash his hair as he put conditioner in his palm then smoothed it through my hair. "We're just not normal." That was all I could think.

He nodded but didn't say a thing. I thought about what had led up to it all. The times flew through my mind. The timid moments in the beginning that rapidly changed into what was our norm.

Would we ever really get to be something we never got a chance to be?

Some people say you have to crawl before you walk, walk before you run, and run before you fly. We'd skipped all the steps. What happens to people who go right to the end?

What would happen to us?

Would we burn out like a flame that burned too bright?

I'd heard of that happening. One could see how an intensity like we had could get hard to take. And then you had the fact that only two months into a relationship we were acting like an old married couple. Did I want things to be that way? And if I didn't, was there a way to change anything?

I didn't know. All I did know was I loved Jett. And he loved me.

After our shower, we dried off and went to get dressed. I pulled a sundress out of the closet as Jett pulled shorts and a t-shirt out of the top drawer. We dressed without saying a word. It was pretty obvious that both of us were thinking about what we could possibly do to fix things. Not that anything felt that wrong, but we both knew things needed to slow way the fuck down.

Just as I finished getting dressed my cell rang. I picked it up off the dresser and saw my sister's name on the screen. "It's Spring." I swiped my finger to answer her call.

Before I could even say hello, she was gushing, "He's here, Asia. We have a boy."

I gasped and sat on the chair closest to me. "A boy!"

"We named him Ray. I know that sounds like a lame name, but there was a single ray of sunshine streaming through the window at the hospital when he came out, and the doctor picked him up. The light hit my baby, and it looked like he was a tiny glowing angel. And his name popped out of my mouth, Ray. My little ray of sunshine."

"How sweet," I cooed. "I can't wait to meet him."

"He can't wait to meet you, Auntie Asia. When can you come? We get out of the hospital later on today. So anytime is cool with us."

I looked at Jett who was trying to look as if he was busy, instead of trying to hear what we were talking about. "I'll check my schedule. It's kind of hectic right now."

Jett looked up at me and shook his head as he frowned and whispered, "You tell her you can go as soon as tomorrow. I'll get you there."

"I hope you can make some time for us, Asia," my sister snapped.

I'd hurt her feelings, although unintentional. "Oh, Spring. I'm kidding. I'll leave tomorrow."

Jett shook his head. "You'll be there tomorrow."

"Oh, I meant to say, I'll be there tomorrow."

"How're are you getting here so quickly?" Spring asked.

"How am I getting there so quickly?" I asked Jett.

"I'll charter you a private jet." He blew a kiss at me.

I thought about leaving him all alone and decided to throw it out there. "Um, Spring, I'm dating someone. Would it be okay if I asked him to join me when I come see you guys?"

"You're dating someone? Is it serious? Is he cute? Did you do it? You know, sex? Has my baby sister finally popped that cherry of hers?"

"God! Spring, really! So, is it okay or what?"

"You better ask him to come too. I have to meet the man who made my little sister a woman."

"For the love of Pete! I'll ask him, and I guess I'll see you tomorrow. How about I bring you dinner. Ribs are still your fav, right?"

"Oh, yes! And potato salad and pinto beans. That would be awesome. Call me when you leave. I love you and so does little Ray. Bye."

Putting down the phone, I eyed Jett who'd overheard it all. "So, will you come with me?"

He came to me, placing his hands on my shoulders as he looked into my eyes. "Asia, do you really want me to come with you? Meet your family? That's a big step you know."

"Uh, are you being serious right now? I mean, I went to your family's vacation. That's a big step." I shook my head as I couldn't believe what he was saying.

"But that was all fake. This is real. Are you sure you want it to get that real? All I've offered you so far is a bunch of phony shit. What you're offering me is as real as it gets."

The smile that lifted my lips to the right felt natural as did my decision. "I want you with me. I like real."

"God, girl. Are we really doing this?"

"If you're game, so am I."

He kissed me with soft lips that spun my world on its axis. "As your boyfriend, I'd be proud to go with you."

So it was set. I was taking Jett to meet the family. I knew they'd all be there, eager to meet the newest addition to the growing brood. And when Spring let them in on my new boyfriend, they'd all be eager to meet him too. I wondered if Jett was ready for all that.

Ready or not, he'd signed up for it, and it was all about to come his way

# 31

# JETT

I had put the wedding rings in the safe at the house before we left the next day to go to South Dakota to see Asia's sister's family. Without them on, as if by magic, things felt different.

The lie took a backseat. So far back, I forgot about it all. Asia and I were feeling more free without that burden. And we were heading to a place where things would be honest.

Well, not entirely honest. They couldn't know I'd bought her and that she was in a Dom/sub contract. And they knew Asia hadn't gone to Los Angeles on vacation. So we were prepared to tell a version of the truth. We met online. A dating site. Then I flew her to Portland where we met up and then flew back to spend the summer at a home I'd purchased not long after she and I started talking.

We'd play the rest of it by ear. But for now, we were living together as boyfriend and girlfriend, exclusive and slowly advancing toward the future. A future we had no preconceived notions about.

I felt pretty good about it. There were some lies, but mostly truths. I suppose we could've told them the entire truth, but Asia said they'd never understand. And she wasn't going to let them know she'd lost her scholarship either.

It became evident that some truths would go untold, but that's life.

Asia held my hand tightly as the plane landed. "Jett, this is so exciting. I've never taken anyone to meet the family. I'm excited and kind of scared too. "

"I am too. I've never been brought to meet the family. This is new for me as well."

Once we got off the jet, I rented a car then we headed to her sister's home, and that's when the nerves kicked in. We were on the doorstep of a modest home in a suburban neighborhood in Sioux Falls, South Dakota. There was one car, an older model sedan, parked in the drive that was cracked with age.

Asia knocked on the door as I wondered how hard things were for them, financially. The home and car showed me they weren't living on high wages. It stoked that fire that had all but burned out in me. The one that told me women only wanted me for my money.

Would Asia ask me to help her sister, brother-in-law, and new nephew out with some money? And if she did, would it change how I felt about her?

The sound of the door opening took me out of my thoughts. A tall man with a big build answered the door. "Asia, my goodness girl!" He pushed the squeaking screen door open and backed up so we could come inside. "And this is your man, huh?" he extended his hand to me. "I'm Max Johnson, welcome to my humble home."

"I'm Jett Simmons. Thank you for allowing me to come to your humble home." I liked the man's handshake. It was firm, short, and friendly.

"Send them back here, baby," came the yell of a woman.

Max hitched a thumb over his left shoulder. "And that's the queen of this castle. Coming, Spring. You guys follow me. The baby's asleep, but he doesn't mind being held while he sleeps."

"Asia tells me this is your first child. How's it going?" I asked as we went through a small dark hallway. There were only three doors coming off it. The house was tiny.

"I have to admit that it hasn't hit me yet. I guess he's too quiet. It doesn't seem real. I'm a dad. At thirty years old, I'm finally a dad." He shook his head and smiled. "Spring and I have been together for five years. This was a long time coming. We just couldn't get the money going right for us. We wanted to wait until we were making good money. We hit some rough times. I worked as a coach at the high school, and she worked at a store as a clerk. This was a busy town when we moved here three years ago. Then it suddenly stopped being so busy, and our jobs vanished. She couldn't find anything, and all I could find was a janitorial job at the jailhouse. But the baby thing wasn't going to wait. The stork came in unannounced."

Another tragic tale of misfortune. I'd heard tons of them. But this man had no idea if I had money or not. Asia hadn't said a word about it. It hit me that people often spoke of their money troubles. It wasn't always directly aimed at getting me to give them anything.

We walked into a small bedroom where her sister, who looked a lot like her, was sitting up, holding a tiny bundle of white. "Hi, guys." Her doe-like eyes, similar to Asia's only Asia's were more beautiful to me, went to me. "And you're Asia's, man. I'm Spring. It's nice to meet you."

"Jett Simmons." I gave her a nod. "It's nice to meet you too."

Asia was quick to take the baby out of her sister's arms as she delivered a kiss to her cheek. "Oh, give him to me." She stepped back next to me. "Oh, my goodness. He's so cute."

Looking down at the baby had my heart speeding up for reasons I couldn't comprehend. Seeing Asia, holding that baby, made her glow in my eyes. "He's a remarkable little guy."

Asia looked at me. "Here, you hold him."

"Me?" I shook my head. "Oh-"

She was quick to get that baby in my arms. Expertly, she maneuvered my arms until I was holding him. "He's so light, isn't he?" Asia asked me.

"He is light. Almost as if I'm not holding anything at all." The baby snuggled against my chest, and the aroma that drifted up to me was like pure Heaven. Baby powder mixed with his brand new smell. "Hi, Ray. It's wonderful to meet you."

"Mom and Dad are on their way up. They'll be here in the morning. You two can have the guest bedroom until they get here, then you can take the sofas in the living room." Spring smoothed out the blanket and straightened her nightgown.

Asia's expression was one of reluctance. "Well, we're not staying here, Spring. We've already gotten a room."

"Oh." Spring looked at me. "I didn't realize that. I mean, that's cool. Usually, my little sister has no money. I'm used to letting her stay with me."

"It's very nice of you to offer. I could get your parents a room there too if you'd like." I nudged Asia. "Mind taking him, baby?"

She took him out of my arms and smiled as she did. "Mom and Dad won't stay anywhere but here, Jett. They're weird about things like that." She cooed at the baby and rubbed noses with him. "He's just so little and precious. I haven't even left yet, and I already miss him."

"You can come as often as you like, Asia," I told her, earning curious expressions from her sister and brother-in-law. "I can make sure she has the means to come see you all. That's what I mean."

"How nice of you," Max said. "Asia, can you take the baby into the living room while I help your sister get into the shower?"

"Sure thing." Asia walked out the door, and I followed her. "Oh, and the food will be delivered in about thirty minutes. I called it in just before we got here."

"Who did you get to deliver?" Spring asked.

"Don't worry about that. Just take a shower, and when you get all done, dinner should be ready to eat." Asia gave her a smile then I closed the door behind us to give them some privacy.

The hotel we checked into had an excellent concierge, even though it wasn't a thing I considered to be a real hotel. The Marriott was one of the most country bumpkin looking hotels I'd ever stayed in. The restaurant was four and a half stars, not bad for South Dakota. They were nice enough, when given a hefty tip, to have the meal of ribs and all the trimmings delivered to us.

Asia sat on the sofa, and I sat next to her. We both looked at the baby, and she sighed. "I love babies. I was there when Bow had her first and third babies. The second was born in the middle of a stormy night. I didn't make it for that one."

"No wonder you look at home with that little guy in your arms. You're an old pro at this aunt stuff." I kissed her cheek. "That looks good on you, by the way."

She blushed, and it sent shots of pure love through me. Asia and that baby were doing something to me. Making me think thoughts I wasn't trying to have. Thoughts about making babies were making me hot.

We'd do dinner with her family then I was going to get my little Asia to the hotel where we could practice making babies all night long.

What the hell had gotten into me? Since when did the idea of babies make me horny?

The shit having Asia in my life had changed was unending. What was next, getting turned on by watching her iron clothes?

32

# ASIA

Jett was crazy by the time we got into our hotel room. He kissed me over and over again as we went up the flight of stairs to our room. Once we were inside, he was ripping my clothes off.

I had no idea what had gotten into him. But I had to admit, I liked it.

"Baby, oh baby, you taste so good. I'm going to eat you up." He chewed on my neck, making my insides melt.

"Jett, what in the world has you so hot?"

He pushed me down on the bed and undressed. He'd already rid me of all my clothing. "You have me hot, baby. I want you. I want you all night long."

His expression was odd. Lusty with a side of love. It was different. I thought maybe the way we'd left the lies behind us had something to do with it. That was until he climbed on top of me and took my hands in his, moving them until they were pinned next to my head. "Jett, why are you just looking at me?"

His eyes roamed all over my face. "You have great bone structure." He moved his hands down to my hips. "You have great round hips too."

"Thank you?" I wasn't sure what he was getting at.

"You're sweet, loving, caring, and fucking adorable when holding a baby in your arms."

Oh shit!

"Jett, what the..." His mouth crashed down on mine as he kissed me like I was his oxygen tank.

He wouldn't let up. He kept kissing me until we both were out of breath. Then he eyed me. "I want to fuck you so hard, and so long you walk wrong for a week."

My head was swimming from the kiss. "K."

"I want you to come so many times, it defies imagination."

"Oh, God!"

"Yeah, baby. Oh, God." He kissed me again and picked me up as he did. He moved around until he was sitting up and then he sat me down on his erection, facing him.

Lifting me up and down, he made my body stroke him. The kiss had to end as I was moving too much. My tits were bouncing everywhere, and he buried his face in them, kissing, sucking, biting. Generally, he was stimulating everything he could, and I was screaming with the pleasure it was giving me.

"I'm about to cum," I told him as the urge hit me.

He flipped me onto my back and thrust back into me. "Do it. I'm coming with you."

Jett's tongue ran up my neck, and he nibbled it as he made forceful thrusts. In no time I was arching up as the wave took me over and he came with me. His groan was deep as he jerked inside me.

He laid still on top of me for a long time. Then he began to move again, his cock going hard inside me. "Oh, you really did mean it when you said you were going to make me walk wrong for a week. I thought that was just some foreplay talk."

"Um hmm." He kept going until he was fully erect again then he flipped me over and took me from behind. He pushed my head and shoulders to the bed then held onto my hips as he went at it.

I was moaning with the arousal. Groaning with the pleasure. Then I was screaming with another orgasm, and he was coming right along for the ride. Filling me once again with his hot juices. He stayed still again as I panted.

After about five minutes, he pulled out and got off the bed. I fell onto it in an exhausted state. "Want some water, Asia?"

"Huh?" My eyes had closed, and I struggled to turn over. "Yeah, I'm thirsty." I managed to sit up, and he came to give me a bottle of water then sat on the bed next to me.

"When would you like to have a baby?"

I nearly choked on the drink. He took it out of my hand as he waited for me to stop coughing, waiting patiently for my answer. "I have no idea, Jett. I've never thought about that."

"Me neither. Not until a while ago." He ran his hand over my stomach. "You'd lookso fucking good with my baby in that belly."

"Jett, we just started dating."

He shook his head. "Don't act like we aren't years ahead of that game, Asia. We have a home together. I take care of you. We could have it all, you and me."

"We can. And one day, maybe we will. But not so soon."

He took a chug of the water, finishing it off, then went to throw the empty bottle away. "You told Mom that we might start having kids soon."

"Yeah, when we were lying about being married, Jett."

He tossed the bottle in the trash then headed back to me. "I know." He laid down next to me and sighed. "I thought I knew how to slow down with you. I guess I don't."

"Learn." I closed my eyes and tried not to think the man was crazy, but it was hard.

"You know, I know this guy from the club, and he paid a sub to have his baby. They didn't know each other at all. They had a baby, and only a few months after he was born they got married. They're like happy as shit now."

"Great," I mumbled as sleep was taking me over. "I'm happy for them. Night, Jett. No baby-talk right now. Love you."

The things billionaires would pay for was staggering. The list just kept growing. Men who'd pay a complete stranger to have their baby? What else would they pay for?

Jett's lips touched my cheek. "Okay, I get it. I do. You need it all. You need a real commitment from me first."

I rolled over to face him and managed to open my eyes. "I don't want a commitment just so you can have a baby. When and if we get to that stage, I want you to ask me to marry you because you can't stand to live without me."

"I see." He kissed the tip of my nose. "Well, I'm probably that way now."

"Probably. See, you don't know yet, and I don't either. Time, Jett. We need some time."

He turned over and closed his eyes. "Fucking time! The root of all evil. Good night. I'll leave you alone about it."

I knew I was right about not having a baby. I knew what I was saying was sane, rational, even very smart. But seeing Jett disappointed was hard to take.

There he was, supposed to be relaxed and falling asleep. Instead, his body was rigid, his arms crossed over his chest, his lips forming a hard line. He was anything but relaxed.

Lying next to him, I could feel the tension radiating off him. I hated it. Easing up to him, I pulled one of his arms around me and laid my head on his broad chest. "I love you."

"I love you." He took in a breath, sniffing my hair. "Get some sleep. We have a long ass day tomorrow it seems. I get to meet the parents. That should be weird."

"Yes, it should. Night."

He was quiet for a minute. But his body wasn't relaxed. I wasn't sure why that was until he whispered, "If you're still awake just nod if you'll think about talking about having a baby in the not too distant future."

What was I supposed to do?

I could act as if I was asleep. He wasn't sure if I was or not. I could nod, but would that be fair to myself?

My plans didn't include babies. Not in the near future, anyway. I knew I wanted kids someday. Not that day, or even year. I had another year of school to get through. And now I had to incorporate Jett into that too. Adding a pregnancy and then a baby to that workload would be stupid and really hard.

But I nodded. I nodded because making Jett happy was what I had done since the get-go. I was his purchase, that was what I was supposed to do. Just because we said some words that were supposed to make that fact go away, it hadn't been erased from my brain.

Do as Jett wants, keep him happy. That's your job.

But that wasn't supposed to really be my job any longer. We were dating. A couple, not a Dom and his sub. Yet, there it was, me nodding to make him happy.

And when he sighed and held me tighter, it made me feel great. I'd made him happy.

Good girl.

But I didn't feel like it was mentally healthy for me to strive to be a good girl. Not if it meant putting my dreams and aspirations to the side to make him or anyone else happy.

I had to do what was right for me. And that was to get through with school and get going on my career before I committed to anything else. A marriage or a baby.

Jett Simmons had some hard facts that would come his way soon. My agenda was important. I had things to do. He was a summer project, meant to fix my financial situation.

It was bad enough I'd fallen in love with a man I was never supposed to. But I wasn't throwing my life away by handing myself over to the man.

Here you go, Jett. Here's my body. Do with it as you want. Put a ring on it. Put a baby in it. Anything you want.

He nuzzled me and whispered, "I wish there was a way to show you how much I love you. I wish there was a way for me to fast-forward time to the place that would be perfect for all I want with you. But there's not. So, all I can do is tell you the words and hope you believe them. We've both told lies, but never to each other. I'm never going to let you go. Not unless you make me."

I tried not to let that sink into my head and affect me. I failed and kissed his chest. "I'll never make you let me go, Jett. I love you. And I know time is a hard thing to take. Especially when you've lived like you're married. But I don't want to go out in a blaze of glory. We burn too hot. I don't want to burn too fast as well."

He kissed the top of my head. "I know. You're right. I'm spoiled rotten."

Maybe he was spoiled. Maybe he was just too used to getting what he wanted when he wanted it. Money could do that to a person.

"Don't talk like that about yourself. You're not spoiled."

"I am, Asia. And I'm bratty, obsessive, compulsive, controlling."

I hated it when he did that. He was so hard on himself. "Sweet, caring, handsome, fun, wonderful, generous."

"I'm not so generous. Where you're concerned, I am. I've never been that way with anyone else. With you, I'm a better man. I don't know how you found that guy inside of me. I never knew he was in there. I've been self-absorbed, self-serving, and just plain selfish. And I'm sorry for trying to force things to move faster. I'll try harder not to do that. That's the selfish man inside of me doing that."

Looking up at him, I found myself sad. "I don't care what you say, I know you're a good man. We're supposed to be going to sleep you know. This isn't the time for reflection."

"Yes, Mom." He kissed me sweetly on my lips. "I'll go to sleep now. And even though I know I shouldn't say this, I will anyway. You're going to make a great mom. Whenever you decide the time is right for that."

With a little smile, I laid my head back on his chest. At first, I felt great. I thought we'd made some good strides. Then I felt kind of shitty. Kind of selfish.

I wasn't thinking like a couple. I was thinking like a single person, the way I always had. His wants, needs, opinions mattered just as much as mine did.

Being a couple was hard to learn how to do. I thought I'd talk to my sisters about it. They'd been married for years. Surely, they'd have some great insight on the subject.

But I couldn't tell them Jett wanted us to have a baby. Not so soon. They'd freak the fuck out.

I was caught in a rough spot. I needed people to talk to but couldn't reveal what Jett and I had really done. The things that made us so close so damn fast.

I'd been dead tired and about to fall asleep. Now I was wide awake and thinking I had no one to talk to about any of this.

How'd I gotten myself into a situation that would be so hard to fucking explain without getting some horrible looks and harsh words? And if I said a thing to my family I could add in mandatory therapy.

I'd really screwed myself!

# 33

# JETT

The drive to Spring and Max's house was hard for me the next day. Asia's parents had arrived, I was about to meet them. The thought of looking her father and mother in the eye, knowing I'd bought their daughter, was eating away at me.

"Okay, so we met online, a dating site." I hit the button to roll the window down. "I need some fresh air."

"Why are you acting so nervous, Jett?" Asia tossed her hair over her shoulder and looked at me like I was crazy. "It's just my parents. They're nice people."

"Oh, I'm sure they are. And I'm not nice people. I'm a man who purchased their daughter from a fucking BDSM club." I wiped sweat off my brow.

"They will never know all that. Stop worrying." She reached into her purse and pulled out some tissues then wiped my forehead. "I've never seen you like this."

Glancing sideways at her, I felt a knot forming in my stomach. "The guilt is getting to me. I can't seem to stop it."

I didn't want to go to that house. I wanted to keep on driving until we got back home. Home, the place where Asia and I could be all alone and not face anyone we didn't want to. A place we could hide away from it all. A place I felt safe with her.

Why did we meet on circumstances that no one could ever know about? Why did I go looking for a fake wife? Why did I take on a sub? Why was I so damn evil?

"Jett, don't let guilt get to you. You've been so nice. You're like the least dominating Dom I've ever heard of."

"That's actually very hurtful to hear. I was a good Dom. I was stern, strict as hell, and I never got emotionally involved with any of my subs or the women at the club I had sessions with."

"I guess you've moved past all that. I suppose you no longer need that since you've found love." She looked out the window and noticed the fact that I was driving right past her sister's house. "Jett, stop! That's it right there."

I put my foot on the brake, slowing to a stop. "Oh." Backing up, I parked next to the curb, hesitating before getting out of the car. My hands gripped the steering wheel.

Asia reached over, laying her hand on top of mine. "It's going to be okay, Jett. I promise you, it will."

The sound of her voice was convincing. The touch of her hand soothed me. The guilt retreated a bit. "I can do this, right? I can look your parents in the eyes. I haven't ever hurt you. I've never made you feel controlled or dominated. I've been good to you."

She nodded. "Yes, you have been very good to me. You can face them. You've never hurt me, Jett. You've only done nice things for me."

Guilt bubbled. "I made you lie."

"I don't think that's so bad. You had your reasons for it. And they don't have to know about all that mess. Here, with my family, you and I are the real versions of ourselves. You can feel free and easy with them. No pretending. Come on. It'll be fine."

Nodding, I had to agree with her. We were mostly on the up and up. "Thanks. You're helpful, baby. Come on then, let's go inside."

Once we stepped out of the car, the front door was flung open, and her mother rushed out to greet us. "There's my baby girl!"

Asia was caught up in her mother's arms as I waited for their hug to end. Then I was caught up in her mother's arms. "Hello," I said as surprise took me over.

"Hello, indeed!" Her mother let me go and held me at arm's length to look me over. "My goodness, Asia, you caught yourself a winner!"

Asia laughed and stole me away from her mother. "Yes, I have. How's our new baby doing today, Mom?"

"Great. He's sleeping." Her mother followed us inside and closed the door behind us.

A large man with tree trunk arms sat on the sofa. He started to get up, but I quickly stopped him. "Hello, you must be Mr. Jones. I'm Jett Simmons, sir. It's an honor to meet you and your lovely wife." I shook his hand and tried not to give off a nervous vibe.

"Jett, nice to meet you." He nodded at his daughter. "Asia, you look well."

She smiled and hugged her father. "Daddy, you do too."

"Asia, can you come here?" her sister called out from her bedroom.

"Coming." She kissed my cheek and hurried away, leaving me all alone with her parents. People who were looking me all over.

"You must work out," her mother said.

I took a seat on the chair in the corner. "I do. Every single morning."

"Did someone teach you how to do that?" her father asked.

"I have a trainer I work with back in Los Angeles. I follow his program." I crossed my legs and put my hands on my knee, not sure what to talk about.

"Max was a coach," her mother said then looked at the hallway.

"Yes, he mentioned that yesterday." I also looked toward the hall, hoping anyone would come out of it and end the awkward conversation I was barely having.

Her father moved around a bit, trying to get comfortable on the old sofa. "I wonder if he could be a trainer."

"I don't see why not. If he knows his way around the human body and all of its muscles, he's a great candidate for the job." I thought I heard the bedroom door open and keened my head, praying someone was joining us.

Her mother whispered, "You should tell Max about that, Jett. He needs some guidance in the job department. I bet he'd listen to you."

"Sure, I'll say something about that."

Then the door did open, and Asia came out, carrying the baby and making my heart do flips. "He's awake, Jett. You'll get to see his eyes."

She came right to me, and I stood up to look at the cute baby.

"Hi there, Ray. It's nice to see you again." I ran my finger over his tiny chin as he looked at me with almond shaped, doe-like eyes. "He's got the Jones' eyes, I see."

"He sure does," her mother agreed.

"He's a handsome kid," her father added.

I caught Asia's eyes as she looked up from her nephew. "He's the first. All of Bow's kids look like their father."

Nuzzling her, I whispered, "I wonder who our kids will look like."

A blush covered her cheeks, making my heart pound.

Take it slow, Jett!

# 34

# ASIA

"We can go pick up things to barbecue, Max. Do you think you could start a fire in the pit in the backyard?" I asked my brother-in-law. Dinner time was approaching, and there was a houseful of people to feed.

"I can do that. Let me grab you guys some cash to buy the food."

Before he could take two steps, Jett stopped him. "I got it, man. It's not a problem. How about some brews to go along with that?"

"That's nice of you. I'd love to toss back a few with you. Hurry back, and I'll teach you how to make a mean chicken leg." Max gave Jett a high-five, and it made me smile.

Jett was getting along well with my family. And when he mentioned something about becoming a personal trainer to Max, I was kind of surprised at how excited Max got about the idea.

When we got to the grocery store, Jett pushed the basket while I grabbed things off the shelf. "I like being all domestic with you, Asia. In fact, I like everything we do together. And I like your family too."

"They sure do like you too, Jett." I wasn't lying. My parents thought he was great. So did my sister and Max. Even the baby felt comfortable in his capable arms.

He moved up beside me, bumping my shoulder with his. "It feels natural. Don't you think?"

I smiled at him and ran my hand over his cheek. "I do."

"I do." He looked at me with soft eyes. "I could say that over and over to you, my little Asia."

I knew what he was getting at. Marriage. A real one.

But I wasn't going to get into that today. I wanted to have a great time with my family. The next day we'd be heading back home to get ready for his high school reunion that would be in Jersey.

Back to one night of lying. I wasn't looking forward to it. Then there'd be a wedding that we'd have to lie at too.

In the back of my mind swirled the fact that if we stayed together, we'd have to eventually come out with the truth. But I didn't want to talk about it yet. I wanted things to settle for us first.

Things were so damn complicated. Maybe too complicated to all work out without things getting very messy. I wasn't sure how we'd pull things off or how people would perceive us if the truth came out. I thought maybe a fake divorce followed by us getting back together might work for his family. But we'd always have problems with getting our families together. A thing both sets of parents were keen on.

That was the first thing my mother said to me, that she wanted to meet his parents. And his parents were set on meeting mine. I didn't know how we were going to handle all that.

Things would have to get messy or worse.

As much as I wanted things to work out, I knew there was a huge chance they wouldn't. It certainly would be easier to walk away after the last function and call it quits. The lie was too big to overcome. My heart, the naïve thing it was, told me anything could be overcome.

The truth will set you free.

That may be so, but that freedom would come at a great cost. No one would look at Jett or me the same way again.

As we stood in the checkout line, Jett ran his arms around me, kissing the side of my head. "I think I might like to do something nice for your sister and her little family, Asia. Do you think giving them a house would be too much?"

I choked on the laugh the came out of me. "Jett, that's too much!"

He nodded. "Yeah, I was afraid you'd say that. But I feel like I could do something to help them get out of the hole they're in. I'm not the kind of person that generally thinks about things like that."

"My family doesn't need you to come in and start throwing money around." I was incensed. "Being poor isn't as bad as it seems to be."

"I didn't mean it like that." He let me go and started to unload the basket onto the conveyor belt. "I'll just leave things alone. I'm sorry."

I was fuming mad and not sure why that was exactly. Jett had money, my family didn't. He was being nice. So why was I so mad? And who was I to tell him he couldn't do something he wanted to?

But I didn't utter one word. I held my tongue. It was far too complicated to talk about or understand. At the simplest form, I didn't want Jett too intertwined with my family. I didn't know what would happen with us after all.

Buying one sister a house, meant he'd soon buy one for my other sister. Mom and Dad would get one too, and that would leave me beholden to the man forever.

No, it was best that I let that lie right where it had fallen. He didn't need to buy any member of my family anything. That was that.

As we loaded the groceries into the car, I noticed how quiet Jett had become. It made me feel bad. "Hey, you know I love you, right?"

He nodded and closed the trunk. "Yeah. You know I didn't mean to overstep any line you had drawn, right?"

With a light laugh, I got into the car, and he did too. "It was a line I didn't know I had. But it's there. It is most definitely there."

"Okay." He started the car. "No big gifts for your family. Got it."

I nodded as he pulled away from the parking lot and headed back. Maybe I was wrong, but the decision felt right. Getting Jett too involved with my family wasn't the right thing to do.

Things were just too up in the air to start things like that.

## 35

# JETT

Driving to Maplewood, New Jersey, I held Asia's hand. Back to the lying, and not feeling good about it. The sun was hanging low in the sky as I drove up to the place we called home before we struck it rich. A modest two bedroom, wood frame home that was once painted white was now bright yellow. "That's it, Asia. That's where I grew up."

"Wow. From that to what you have now. Crazy, huh?" She shook her head as she looked at the small home. "And all because your mother came up with a great recipe and your dad figured out how to sell it. The American dream."

The memories the old house stirred were filling my head. Soon, I'd be seeing people I grew up with. People who knew me before I was the man I became.

I had dressed down, not wanting to attract any attention to my financial status. That night I wanted to be plain old Jett from down the street.

Asia ran her hand over my arm. "Feeling a bit melancholy?"

The engagement ring and wedding band on her finger took my attention. I took her hand and kissed those rings. "I am. And I feel like things need to change. I'm a fake, Asia. A big fat phony."

She looked at the rings too and sighed. "If I knew what to do, I'd tell you. But I don't. Not without making us look like liars."

"Which I am. You're not one. I made you do it." I looked down as I shook my head.

I needed to get out of it all. But no idea that I'd come up with would work without leaving me in another boat full of lies or with egg on my face.

As hard as it was to think about, the only thing that would work was my original plan. A fake divorce. That would mean leaving Asia alone for a period of time. A thing I didn't want to do.

As I pulled up at my old high school gym, I saw people walking into the double doors that I barely recognized. "Fuck, we're all so old."

"It's only been ten years, Jett. You guys are still young. Come on. I can't wait to meet your old friends. I bet they've got all kinds of stories to tell on you." Asia got out of the car, looking excited.

I got out, feeling depressed.

We walked up to the doors, hand in hand as I prepared myself for what was to come. A girl I didn't recognize but saw her name tag said Julie, was sitting at a small desk. "Hi, Jett. It's been a long time since I've seen you. And this is your wife, I see. Sign in and fill out your names on the tags there and put them on your shirt, like I've done."

"Hi, Julie. How are you?" I had no idea who the hell she was. But I knew I had gone to school with her. I guess I was pretty self-absorbed back then too.

After putting on our name tags, we headed through the next set of doors and found a bunch of people standing around in small groups.

"Wow, so this is what a high school reunion is really like." Asia looked around at everyone. "Kind of depressing how much it's like when you were in high school, huh? Everyone is in their old cliques."

And they were too. My little group was gathered around the punch table. "Come on. That's mine over there, sipping punch that's bound to be spiked already." I took Asia by the hand and led her to meet my old friends.

"Hey, Jett!" the sound of a familiar female voice called out.

"Fuck," I muttered then turned around. "Sandy."

My old girlfriend was making her way to me. She'd put on the pounds and was followed by a man who was already going bald. "And she is?" Asia whispered.

"My high school girlfriend."

"Oh, wow!"

"Yeah."

Sandy was all smiles as she came up to me, demanding a hug and leaving a kiss on my cheek. "Oh, Jett, you look so good."

"You too, Sandy." With all the lies I'd be telling that night, what would one more hurt?

"Thanks. This is my husband, Doug. And who's this?"

I put my arm around Asia. "This is Asia, my wife."

Asia gave them nods. "Nice to meet you, Sandy, Doug."

Sandy's face fell. "I hadn't heard you got married. When did this happen?"

"At the beginning of summer." I looked past her and her hubby to see my friends making goofy signs at me. I guess they thought my old girlfriend coming up to me was amusing.

Juveniles.

"Oh, so you two are newlyweds then?" Sandy asked as she smiled. "Well, congrats you guys. Doug and I've been married for years. I met him right after high school. We have four kids." She patted Doug on the back as if he'd done a great job at getting her knocked up so many times. "We just love our family. Doug, take out your cell, show Jett our kids."

The dutiful husband took out his phone and handed it to me. "Dave, Donald, Davin, and Darla. That's them there."

I looked the photo over then handed him his phone back. "Great looking kids you two have there." I lifted my chin in gesture to my group. "Looks like my buds are calling me. Glad to see you and glad things are going great for you, Sandy."

"You too, Jett. Nice to meet you, Asia."

Walking away, I felt relief that was over. "She's nice." Asia looked back over her shoulder at Sandy. "What happened to end it?"

"She tried to trap me into marriage by poking holes in my condoms."

"Oh, shit!" Asia laughed. "Wow. People really do that?"

"She did. Lucky for me I caught on to what she'd done before anything happened that would've ruined my life." I got to the guys I called friends what seemed like a hundred years ago. "Hey, way to help a man out, guys."

"What?" Josh asked as he laughed. "Sandy ambush you, bro?"

"Yeah, yeah." I took the punch he handed me as another old friend patted me on the back. "Hey, Todd. How're things?"

"Like always. They're going along as good as they can. And you? Is this your wife?" Todd handed her a drink too.

"Oh, yeah. Asia, these are my oldest friends. That's Josh, this is Todd, those two over there are Larry and Clyde. Guys, meet Asia."

She smiled at them all. "I bet you have great stories about this guy here. I'm up for hearing them all."

Josh pulled his wife away from the punch bowl and her chatting with the other wives. "This is Tammy, Asia. My wife. She's been trying to set Jett up for years. But she never came up with anyone as pretty as you are."

Tammy shook Asia's hand. "It's great to meet you, Asia. I don't know how you managed to get this guy to marry you, but you're one crafty woman. I couldn't even get him to date anyone."

"Yes, he's very picky." Asia ran her arm around me, and I ran mine around her then kissed her cheek.

"I am picky. When I found her, I scooped her up and made her my wife as quickly as she'd let me."

Tammy nodded. "Any plans for kids yet?"

"Yes," I said.

"No," Asia said.

Everyone laughed, except me. I wanted a baby. I wanted one with Asia so bad it was nearly all I could think about. And she had shut me down about it. I wasn't used to being shut down. I didn't like it.

Josh showed me pictures of his two kids and glowed with pride. The other guys all had kids too. I was the only one with a fake wife and no kids. I was pathetic.

The lights went low, and music began to play. I swept Asia into the middle of the floor to dance with her and get away from the others.

"You didn't have to be so honest about the kid thing, Asia."

"Well, I'm sorry, it just kind of blurted out of me."

"Don't you see how they all have wives and families and I have nothing? It's embarrassing. Humiliating."

"You're being dramatic. I'm sure some of the people here aren't married with kids. There's no rush to do all that, Jett."

"If there's not then why do I feel like there is? Why do I feel as if I've been doing shit wrong my whole life? Now, I've missed out on things my friends have already experienced?"

"You'll get those experiences too, one day." She leaned her head on my shoulder. "Time Jett, remember?"

"Oh yes, how can I forget about the elusive time that you want so much of."

I was mad. Hurt. And feeling done.

With what, I didn't know. But I felt like I wanted things to be done. One way or another, I wanted things to end. The lie, the love, something needed to stop.

Her hand moved to cup the back of my neck as she looked into my eyes. "We have one more thing to get through, Jett. Then you and I will sit down and figure out what we're going to do."

I had no idea when I lost all control. But I had lost it. Asia was telling me how things were going to be. I was going through the damn motions.

"Asia, I don't like this."

"Me neither."

"No, I mean I don't like you acting as if you're in charge here. I'm still in charge." I shouldn't have even have had to tell her that. "We still have a contract."

"Yes, we do. And I'm doing what you want me to."

A force was pushing me that I seemed unable to control. I took her out of the gym, away from everyone. Leading her out to the football field, I leaned her against the fence that surrounded it. "I might want you to get into another contract with me. One with more stipulations.

This freedom thing isn't setting well with me. I want you, Asia. It would mean more money for you if you agreed to one."

Her soft hands caressed my face as she looked at me with love in her eyes. "Jett, I'm not about to get into any more contracts with you or anyone ever again. You've taught me that I'm not the kind of woman who can live that way. I don't want any more of your money. I want to be with you, but I want to be free. Free to be with you on our terms. Not some contract's terms. Do you understand?"

I did understand. I knew then and there, she was perfect for me.

I didn't realize it myself until she gave me the right answer. Asia wasn't using me for my money. She wanted my heart, and that's all she wanted.

Holding her chin, I ran my thumb over her lips. "Asia, you're the one, baby. You're her."

She was perfect for me. I knew I'd do everything I could to make her mine in name. She didn't stand a chance of not becoming Mrs. Jett Simmons for real.

# 36

# ASIA

The night had been long, full of funny stories about Jett and his friends. I felt like I knew Jett a hell of a lot better after meeting the people he called friends in his younger days. I also felt like Jett wanted to move forward with me a lot faster than I thought was smart.

Another thing I could blame on the fake marriage.

As we made the ride back home the next day, Jett was in a rambunctious mood. “If I took you to the airport and we took off to Las Vegas what would you think?”

“I’m not doing that today, Jett.”

He looked at me as he pulled up to a stop light. “You know, there are tons of women who’d jump at the chance to marry a handsome billionaire.”

“I do know that.” I ran my hand over his shoulder. “But you don’t love any of them. You love me. And I want to go slow.” My cell rang, and I saw my mother’s name on the screen. “It’s Mom.” I swiped the screen. “Hi, Mom.”

“Hey, baby girl Guess where your father and I happen to be?”

“Where?”

“Harrison. We thought we’d stop by.”

"Oh, I see." I looked at Jett, and he just smiled.

"Tell them we'll be home in about thirty minutes and text them the address."

I could tell he was happy about their visit. "Mom, I'll text you the address. Give us a half hour to get home."

"Sure thing. Bye."

I put my cell down and pinched the bridge of my nose. "I don't like this."

"What? Your parents stopping by. I love it. It means they feel comfortable about us. Don't you think so?" He ran his hand over my knee.

"And now they'll know how much money you have and how you've bought me a car and expensive clothes. Jet, this is bad."

I couldn't see how he didn't understand that. There'd be tons of questions, and all of our answers would have to be made up. On the fly too. We'd have to work to keep our answers the same.

"It's okay, baby. Just tell them the truth about things. I asked you to move in. I gave you a car to drive and some clothes to wear. You don't have to tell them the house is yours." He gave my leg a pat, much like one would do to a dog.

Maybe he was right. Maybe they wouldn't freak out too much. We already said we were spending the summer together. At least part of it was out there. But I had no idea how they'd react to Jett being filthy rich and me leaving all that out.

They didn't know we went to South Dakota in a private jet. The car Jett rented was just a typical small car, nothing fancy. We wore shorts and t-shirts, nothing upscale. I knew they'd be shocked.

When they asked Jett what he did for a living, he downplayed it by saying he was in management. That might come off as lying to my parents. I guess we'd soon find out because traffic was light for once and we were nearly home.

"My stomach hurts," I whined.

"It'll be okay." Jett chuckled. "If I'm nervous, you're not and vice versa. That's funny."

"Nothing is funny about how badly my stomach is hurting. I don't know if it's nerves or that damn jungle juice punch we drank last night, but it's cramping pretty badly." I held my poor tummy all the rest of the way home. I had to make a mad dash to the first bathroom, once we got there.

Puking my guts up had me thinking it had to be the punch, not nerves. I rinsed out my mouth and went to find Jett putting our bags in the bedroom. "Your friends poisoned me."

"Here, lie down, baby." He came to me and made me lean on him as he took me to the bed. "Did you have a headache that you didn't tell me about? You know, signs of a hangover?"

"No. It just hit me all of a sudden. My stomach doesn't hurt anymore. I feel a little weak, but other than that, the cramping is gone." I ran my hand over my stomach. "Maybe I just had to get it out of me."

"I guess so. I'll go get you some ginger ale. That might help." He walked away, and I sat up as the bell to the gate rang. He smiled at me. "They're here."

I sighed then got up. No time to rest and get back to feeling a hundred percent, I guessed. "Crap."

Jett ran his arm around me. "That's no way to feel about your parents coming over. Should I call in? You know, have some lunch delivered?"

"I guess so."

"I'll do that while you entertain them. Show them all around." Jett gave my shoulders a squeeze. "Invite them to stay over tonight."

"Are you sure about all that?" I shook my head.

"Of course I'm sure. I want them to feel at home here." We walked to the keypad in the living room, and he punched in the code to the gate then opened the front door.

We stood there, waiting to see my parents old Buick come up the drive. "If they freak out, then I'll tell them that's why we didn't tell them that you're rich. There, I feel better about it all now."

"Good." He hugged me tight and then his arms went loose. "Fuck me. It's my parents."

Right behind the BMW Jett's parents were in was my father's old car.

"Fuck me! Jett, what the fuck are we going to do?"

"All that comes to mind is, run."

"Why the fuck did we come to the door? We could've hidden inside from them. We're totally fucked." I couldn't take in any air. My heart had stopped beating.

I looked at my hand and realized we still had on our wedding bands. There was only one thing to do. It would be hard to do, but we had no choice.

There wasn't time to think, to plan, to hightail it out of there and run to Canada where they'd never find us. So I took a deep breath and waved with a happy smile on my face. Then I took Jett's hand in mine and stepped off the first step. "Follow my lead, Jett."

"Okay. Shit, I hope you have something great planned."

# 37

# JETT

Each step we took toward the people who knew different stories was excruciating. My ears were ringing, my gut was twisting, and I couldn't think at all. But it seemed Asia could.

She took my hand and led the way as well as the plan that came into her head at record speed. My parents got out of the back of the car.

"Hi, OMG! What a surprise, you guys." Asia let my hand go and hugged my mother. "Okay, I have a confession to make."

My knees went weak.

What was she doing?

Mom's brows went up. "About what, dear?"

"The people behind you guys are my parents. And I made Jett lie for me. I'm really sorry." Asia held my mother's hands. "I know we told you that they knew about our marriage. They don't know a thing about it. I've been too afraid to tell them."

Mom smiled. It had worked. My mother loved being in the know about things. "I understand, perfectly. It was rushed and quite unexpected."

"Thank you for understanding. It means the world to me."

I was relieved and could finally take a breath. I watched Asia's parents get out of their car and jogged up to greet them. "Hi there. We have a couple of surprise guests today. My parents dropped in as well. You'll all get to meet, the way you wanted."

Asia brought my parents along with her to make the introductions. And I had to hand it to her parents, they weren't freaking out about the lavish home. Her mother looked around. "This is very nice, Jett. You've done well for yourself, haven't you?"

"Well, my parents can give you the run down on why we've become successful." I turned to take Asia's hand as she came up beside me. She grabbed my right hand with her left and held up our clasped hands. Her rings caught the sun, glistening and making me nearly choke. Then she said something that made me feel lightheaded.

"Okay, we're busted. Mom, Dad, Jett wanted to tell you guys right away, but I wouldn't let him. I was afraid of how you'd react. He and I were married In Vegas on the first of June."

"Asia," I hissed. "No."

She looked at me with a smile. "It's okay, Jett. I'm ready to let them in on our secret. No more lies will come out of me."

I looked from her to her parents to find them slack-jawed and wide-eyed. Her father cleared his throat and looked at my father. "Did you know about this?"

My parents nodded, and Asia's looked at one another. Her mother nodded. "Okay, okay. You were right, Asia. We most likely would've overreacted." She fanned herself.

Moving quickly, I headed toward the house. "Come inside. Sit down, I'll get you something to drink. I know you must be stunned."

They were probably just about as stunned as I was. I couldn't believe what Asia had done for me. It was too much.

Asia made sure everyone got inside as I went to grab some wine and hard liquor. I needed a drink and fast.

Gulping down a glass of Scotch, I refilled it then took the wine and some glasses to the den where Asia had settled everyone. I found Asia showing her parents the wedding rings and smiling away as she told them that she also lied about how we met, a thing she also made me do. "You see, I'd sneaked away with Joy to Los Angeles. I didn't want you guys to know I did that. And I'm sorry. I really am. I didn't think about what I was doing. I don't know why I thought the truth would never catch up to me, but I didn't. Can you guys ever forgive me?"

Her father looked at me with a frown. "In the future, could you please help our daughter to be more honest with us?"

I fell on the sofa and nodded as I took another drink. The guilt was trying to take over. I wanted to tell everyone it was me who was the huge liar. Asia was an innocent victim in my scam.

But she'd thrown herself on the sword, so to speak. How could I turn her virtuous sacrifice into just another pack of lies?

I couldn't do that to her. But I'd do anything to make things up to her. Anything at all.

The hard part was figuring out what I'd need to do to rid myself of the tremendous guilt. Asia was taking the blame for everything when she wasn't to blame for one damn thing.

I gulped my drink down. "I'm going to go call in something for lunch."

"That sounds fantastic, son." Mom waved at me as I left the room full of cheerful people. I walked to the kitchen to find the take out menus we'd accumulated since moving in.

Pulling up a bar stool at the island, I looked through the things then felt a warm hand on my back. "You okay?"

I turned around and saw Asia's sweet face. "You shouldn't have. I could've just told the truth."

She shook her head. "No, I couldn't let you do that. My way was easier. We'll figure things out later. For now, we're back to being fake married in everyone's eyes. If I'd never gone to South Dakota, we'd never have been in this situation. I had to do it. I had to keep up our deal."

"I'm sorry, Asia. I truly am. Is there anything I can do for you? I'll do anything at all that you want. You want a beach house in Malibu? I happen to have one of those. It's yours, baby."

She ran her arms around me and rubbed her nose against mine. "All I want is your love, Jett. That's all I'll ever need."

"I could really make you my wife." I held my breath, hoping she'd agree.

"No."

With one word, she shut me down again. "Okay. I won't argue with you about that. I won't argue with you about a thing. Not after what you've done for me. I know that wasn't easy."

"Well, it wasn't that hard."

She wasn't fooling me. I knew she wasn't a liar. I knew she would never intentionally tell her family lies. I'd made that happen. Now Asia wasn't only lying to strangers she never had to have anything to do with again if she didn't want to. Now she was lying to the people who'd always be in her life.

I'd taken her down a bad road that was leading us both into sinful territory. I was making her credibility something people would question if the truth ever came out.

But she didn't seem to care at that moment. She kissed me and told me everything would be alright. Things would work out. And I believed her.

Don't ask me how I did. The web of lies I had going on just kept getting thicker. Stickier. Trapping us in a situation.

I didn't want to feel trapped, and I definitely didn't want Asia to feel that way. I wanted our love to be free. But I was beginning to wonder if it would ever be that way.

"Asia, if I could go all the way back to the first time I saw your sweet face on that website and talked to you, I'd change so many things." I kissed her back.

She leaned her head against mine. "Hindsight is twenty, twenty, people say. What's done is done. We can't change a thing we've done."

"I feel like we're stuck."

She nodded. "Yeah. It's kind of like the glue that will hold us together, or it might just muck everything up. I guess we'll find out with time which it is."

Mom came into the kitchen and gave a quick clap to let us know she was there. "Hey, we had a great idea. Let's all go out and eat. Your Dad and I are treating. And I wanted to remind you that you need to get with our human resource department and get Asia on your insurance plan. Have you taken her to the banks to get on your accounts? You'll need to do all that too. As your wife, she needs that protection. If something happens to you, she'll have a hell of a time getting through all that paperwork. You're married now. You have lots to make sure gets done."

I looked at Asia, and she smiled at me then at my mother. "We'll have to get busy with that then, won't we?"

It became crystal clear. I hadn't thought anything through at all. Maybe I wasn't as smart as I'd always thought I was.

It seemed so simple. One little lie would keep me from being hassled this summer about finding a girl and getting serious.

Boy, that one went south on me!

# 38

## ASIA

So I'd done it. I'd stomped right in and told my family a bunch of crap just to make sure I kept up the sham for Jett. He didn't ask me to. I knew he'd never ask me to do a thing like that.

But it was there, deep inside of me.

Keep Jett happy.

The money wasn't the issue. Not the driving force that had me making that drastic decision. It was my love for him that forced me to do a thing I'd never even considered doing.

As we drove back from lunch, our parents all heading to their own homes, Jett and I held hands. My stomach was full of the Italian food we'd eaten. I was sleepy and in a daze.

Jett would marry me if I wanted. So why wasn't I hopping on that as fast as I could?

Resting my head on the headrest, I turned to look at the gorgeous man who was driving. Jett was a masterpiece of a man. His dark hair, hanging in silky waves to his broad shoulders. A pair of Ray Ban aviators made him look hot and sexy. He was it. The complete package.

Was I mental or something?

I mean, if I was to go back to college and show my friends a picture of this man and told them, yeah he asked me to marry him, and I was like, no way, dude. They'd call the 911 and tell them I was in need of a brain transplant, STAT.

It whirled around in my head and came out of my mouth, "Jett, marriage is sacred to me. Like, I don't ever want to get a divorce. My Aunt Shirley got a divorce. She and her husband had three kids, a dog, and a pet goat. When their marriage ended, the whole lot of them went downhill. The house, goat, and dog, vanished. The kids turned into delinquents. My aunt became a bit of a tramp, and my uncle wasn't spoken about or seen again."

"It is scary. And just so you know, I don't take it lightly either. But I'm not going to ask you about that for a while. I respect the hell out of what you did for me today. I wouldn't dare bother you about anything." He gave me a smile. "You've gone above and beyond for me. Way past anything a typical sub would do. I may not have put you through the typical tests one puts a sub through, but I've tested your limits plenty. You've surpassed all of my expectations. And sexually, well you know you rock me, baby."

So there it was, he wasn't going to ask me to marry him for a while. I should've felt great. Relieved.

If that was how I was supposed to feel then why did I have an empty spot inside me that was growing by leaps and bounds? And it happened so suddenly.

The feelings I was having told me one thing. I was being bratty. At first, I was all, no Jett, I don't want to get married. We need time. Then he tells me he'll give me time and I'm all, what?

I felt like an idiot for getting what I had asked for and not wanting what I got.

I kept quiet, not wanting to let Jett in on the emotional roller coaster I was on. He held my hand all the way home and into the house. It was early, yet I was feeling tired for some reason. All the stress, I guessed.

"Hey, wanna take a late nap with me?" I asked him.

"I'm not tired in the least." He ran his arm around my shoulder. "But I could watch some television and hold you while you get some rest if you'd like."

"Nah, I want some peace and quiet. I'll go up to our room, and you can watch television in the media room downstairs."

With a kiss, we parted ways, and I went to bed. I barely laid my head on the pillow before I was in a deep sleep.

I had no idea how much time had passed before I was woken up by a sharp pain in my stomach. Rushing to the bathroom, I blew chunks in the toilet. A cold sweat broke out all over me, and I was shaking as I hugged the toilet.

I managed to pull myself together as I washed my face, cooling myself down. In the mirror, I saw my reflection. I had dark circles under my eyes, even though I'd just gotten some sleep. Was I coming down with a virus?

Little by little, the nausea went away, and I felt perfectly fine. Great, actually.

Making my way to the media room, I found Jett lounging on the sofa. He was watching sports and drinking a beer. "Hey, you."

He turned to look at me. "Hey, baby. You get your nap?"

I sat down next to him and nodded. "Yeah. I feel much better." I decided to leave out the part about getting sick again. I didn't want him to get concerned. "So, basketball, huh? You like sports?"

"Ah, I can take them or leave them. Not a crazy fan of any one team. I just like to watch the games now and then so I can keep up with things. You wanna do something?"

I was actually feeling quite horny but wasn't sure how to approach him with that. "Wanna take a swim?"

"Sure. Let's go change." He got up and took my hand, but I pulled him back.

"Wanna skinny dip?"

He smiled at me and nodded. "With you, anytime."

Quickly, we went out to the pool and ditched our clothes then jumped into the cool water. I felt free as we swam around each other in circles. I made sure to tease him, staying just out of his reach.

He made a quick grab for me, and I let him catch me. "Oh, no," I giggled. "What will you do with me now?"

His sea green eyes danced. "Anything I damn well want to."

Desire shot through me like a lightning bolt. “I am yours.”

Pressing me against the side of the pool, I ran my legs around him, urging him to enter me. He did as I wanted, giving me the long, thick part of him that I was craving.

Sparks shot through me as I moaned and leaned my head on his shoulder as he moved me. Being connected to him was the best feeling I ever had. Somehow, with him in that way, I felt more alive than I ever had. Each and every time we made love, it just got deeper and deeper, what I felt for him.

His kiss sent me spiraling down, unaware of anything but how his body felt, moving with mine. It was blissfully slow and steady and when the wave inside me crested, I moaned, “Jett, I love you so much.” Then the wave crashed, and he groaned as he released too. “Baby, I love you too.”

We were still for a while, just holding one another. I rested my head on his shoulder as he ran his fingers lightly over my back. We didn’t need to say a thing to convey what we felt for each other. It was all there in our bodies. It was then that I knew I’d kill for the man. I’d do anything in the world for him. So what was I waiting for?

“Jett?”

“Yeah, baby?”

I pulled back to look at him, gazing into his eyes. “Do you really want to marry me?”

He pressed his finger to my lips. “Hush. I know I’ve been pushy about that. I know that you’ll do anything I want. And I don’t want you to marry me just because I want it. I’d like you to want it too. As a matter of fact, I don’t want to marry you right now. Not because I don’t love you. I love you more than I knew I could love anyone. But because I’ve seen that you are completely selfless where I’m concerned.”

All I could do was nod and rest my head on his shoulder again. He no longer wanted to marry me. I had no idea when he’d want to or if he’d want to.

Maybe my selfless act was a bad thing for us. Maybe I was giving too much of myself to him. I wasn’t sure if I’d done the right thing. But it was done. I was in as deep as he was in the fake marriage.

There was a niggling notion in the back of my mind. One that said the fake marriage and the tower of lies would crumble, leaving us in the rubble of it all.

A tear slipped out of my eye as I held Jett tight in my arms, never wanting to let him go. Maybe if I just held on, things would never end. Nothing would change. He and I would become just like the other statues that highlighted our large yard. Frozen in time, the lovers who were doomed if they made any movements.

Like all things, that moment had to end. "I think we should think about eating dinner, Asia. What do you say to Chinese?"

My stomach growled at the thought, and he moved me in his arms, taking me out of the water. "I think my tummy is saying, yes."

He chuckled as he grabbed a couple of towels and handed one to me. I wrapped it around me and followed him inside. All the while watching him as he strode along in front of me. And all the while wondering if I'd done the right thing.

But what else could we have done in the situation?

I had no idea what the answer to that was. I also had no idea what we'd do to make things legitimate. It seemed neither of us had an answer for that question.

# 39

# JETT

As I watched Asia sleep the night before the wedding that would've been our last social occasion together, I felt that guilt that had come to be my constant companion. It moved like hot lava through me. Letting me know I had taken an innocent young woman and morphed her into something else. Something I didn't want her to be.

Asia had become my fierce protector. Which sounds like a good thing, until you really think about it. She would hurt herself just to save me. I didn't want her to do that.

I was a man who should be facing his mistakes and dealing with them. Not hiding behind lies and a girl to protect myself from feeling shame.

I needed to feel ashamed of what I'd done. I deserved to feel that ominous weight. I'd done wrong. I'd taken a person, made them lie for me to everyone, including her own family. And what was the absolute worst, she did it on her own to save my sorry ass.

Asia deserved a good man. And I wasn't a good man. I was bad. I supposed I'd always be bad. Morally unsound, mentally incapable of changing.

Our time was limited. Even though we loved each other with everything we had in us, it had to end. I wasn't good for her.

I knew she'd never agree to breaking up. She'd cry, demand that I stop being crazy. And most likely convince me that we could figure a way out of the lies and bring what was real between us out into the open.

But I knew that people would wonder why she did it. Because I would wonder that too. That's when the whole Dom/sub contract thing would come out, ruining Asia's life for good.

No one would look at her the same way again. Her family were good people. They'd never understand why she did such a thing. And they'd look at me like the dirt-bag I was. And they'd be right to think of me in that way.

Money is why Asia came to me, and she'd have plenty. She'd have a house, a car, a closet full of expensive clothes. She'd be upset by my leaving, but she'd get over it.

Eventually.

And I would too, wouldn't I?

I was doing it out of my immense love for her after all. It was the only selfless thing I'd ever do. But it did nag at me that she'd be hurt by my selfless act.

But she'd be hurt if the truth about us came out too.

Asia was going to be hurt no matter what happened. She was a casualty in every way. I'd wreck her life any way I went.

I'd never felt more alone in the world. I'd never felt so sad and depressed while feeling so much love it hurt. It was the oddest of times and feelings.

Asia stirred, opened her eyes and found me looking down at her. "Jett, what in the world are you doing?"

"Just looking at how beautiful you are when you're sleeping peacefully." I pushed her hair off her face and kissed her cheek. "So, tomorrow is the last of the fake marriage. I'm just mulling over how I feel about that."

"It can't be the last of it. We'll have to figure something out. Our families think we're married too. Don't worry about it. Just go to sleep. When the time is right, one of us will come up with an idea that'll work. Have faith. I do." She snuggled down under the blanket and closed her eyes.

Should I say something to give her a hint as to what I had figured out about fixing the fake marriage problem?

She looked peaceful again, and I knew I couldn't tell her a thing. If she had any idea about what I was planning, she'd fight me like a badger. That was one of the best things about Asia. She wasn't afraid of a fight.

But I wasn't going to have a fight over what I knew was the right thing to do by her. I told her from the very beginning that I'd do right by her and I meant to keep my word.

Her breathing was steady, she had fallen back to sleep. I knew I should be getting some rest too, but I couldn't stop looking at her. I'd leave her alone the very next night if things went the way I thought they would.

She'd wake up alone and find my note. The one I'd leave her to explain to our families what had happened to me. The one that would set her free from all these lies.

Perhaps one day in the distant future I could come back to see if things could blossom between us again. But I wasn't sure about that. What I would do would hurt her to the core. I knew that.

That was a weight I'd have to take on. She was worth that. I was carrying around guilt anyway, why should I get to live life without any weight of that on my shoulders?

Asia didn't need me in her life. I would just be a reminder of when she walked on the dark side for a while. She'd be better off without me.

No, I'd walk away and never come back. That would be the right thing to do. Leave her for good. It would be better that way.

Settling my head on the pillow, I closed my eyes, willing myself not to think about it anymore. I'd never leave if I thought about it too much. And I had to leave. For Asia's sake, I had to do it.

Just as I got my mind to shut up, Asia threw the blankets off her and bolted to the bathroom. I got up and followed her, finding her with her head in the toilet, puking her guts up. "Baby?" I held her hair back as I knelt beside her.

She wretched over and over, getting rid of everything that was in her stomach. Then she moaned and sat on the floor with her face in her hands. "God, I don't know what's wrong with me, Jett."

I got up and grabbed her a wet washcloth. Then I picked her up and sat her on top of the vanity. Wiping her face with the cool cloth, I felt her shaking.

Neither of us had a thing on as we slept naked each night. I picked her up and took her to bed, covering her up and running my hand over her forehead. "You don't have a fever. You didn't say your stomach was hurting."

"It just hit me. I was fast asleep, then I was up and running. That's the third time today."

"I'll take you to the doctor tomorrow. I'll let my family know we won't be going to the wedding."

"Jett, no. I'll be alright. It's probably a little stomach bug. You know a twenty-four-hour thing. Just get back into bed. I'll be better by the morning. You'll see."

I got back into bed, unsure that it was a stomach bug that was causing her to be fine one moment and throwing up the next. Something was wrong, and I was pretty sure I knew what it was.

Stress.

The stress of lying to her family was too much for her. Her brain thought she could handle it. Her body was rejecting it.

I could see it clear as day even if she couldn't. The lies were getting to her, making her sick.

I had to leave. I wasn't healthy for her. Not in any way.

But I held her that night. For the rest of the night, I clung to her and wished like hell there was another way to make things right. I fell asleep with no other idea in my head.

I had to go. I owed it to her.

## 40

# ASIA

In the month of August, I'd thrown up more than I had in my entire life. Much of the time, Jett knew nothing about it. I didn't want him to worry about me.

I was pretty sure it was stress-related. I thought all the time about what we could do to make things right. It was always there, knocking at my brain.

If I'd been a liar my whole life, I think that would've helped me to deal with what I'd done. Lies apparently did not sit well with me. Hence the vomiting.

Jett was being bothersome, nagging me to go to the doctor. We had one more wedding to go to, and I wasn't about to mess that up for him. I promised I'd go the next day if I got sick any more.

I had a couple bouts of nausea throughout the day, but nothing too bad. Maybe with the last wedding to attend, the stress would ease up. I hoped so anyway.

The fact was that I wanted to talk to Jett about really getting married. Wouldn't that end all our problems?

We could simply go to Vegas and do it for real, and then no one had to know anything else. If Jett would agree, I thought the stress would vanish.

I hoped it would, and I hoped he'd agree. His notion of me wanting to marry him only because it was something he wanted and I wanted to please him, was stupid.

I loved the man!

I loved Jett more than I knew was possible. And I did want to marry him. The main reason was love. The other reason was to get the lie over with. We'd be married, and all that nonsense of a fake marriage would be over.

There was one easy fix. The hard part was getting Jett to accept the easy fix.

It was crazy, the man had wanted to marry me, and I had to be bullheaded about it. Then I want to get married, and he got stubborn about it.

It was funny, really. Only it was time for the joke to be over and for us to take the bull by the horns and take charge of the situation.

Stop the lie by really getting married.

It was the only way to go. The only thing in my way of fixing it all was Jett. Now how would I get him to see reason.

# 41

# JETT

Our last social function was at hand. My cousin, Felicity and her fiancé, Ron had put on a fancy wedding at The Plaza Hotel in New York. My parents insisted we all get rooms there and stay the night. It trumped my plans for leaving that night.

I'd get one more night with Asia. That was both good and bad. Every minute I spent with her made it that much harder for me to leave. Doing the right thing was getting harder and harder to do.

The damn wedding wasn't making things any easier, either. Holding Asia's hand, we watched the bride go to meet her groom, and my heart ached that Asia and I'd never get that moment.

She gave my hand a squeeze. "She looks amazing."

I leaned in to whisper. "You'd look better."

Taking her eyes off my cousin to look at me, she smiled. I couldn't take my eyes off hers. Our connection was deep and true. And I was a fool for what I'd done. But nothing could change it.

The music stopped, and we all sat back down. I ran my arm around Asia. She rested her head on my shoulder, and we watched the rest of the wedding play out.

There was a dinner that was held elsewhere then it would be back to The Plaza for the reception. Asia and I rode with my parents in their limo to that part of the event. Mom chatted away after we all got into the car, "Wasn't that lovely? How I wish we could've done something like that for you two."

Asia sighed. "As lovely as that was, I'd never want anything that large anyway. All this seems like a lot of trouble to go through to me."

I wrapped my arm around her and kissed the side of her head. "I agree. I think it would've been nice to have had our families with us when we got married, but no one else."

"Yes, keeping it informal and small would've been good." Asia leaned her head on my shoulder. "Plus, I'm worn out just by attending. What must the bride and groom feel like?"

Mom's expression grew to one of concern. "Asia, dear, have you been doing okay? I only ask because you seem to have lost weight since I saw you last."

"She's been a little under the weather," I answered for her.

Asia nodded. "Although living with your son has been the best, I have a lot of worry over school. I failed two classes last semester and that has me worried about retaking them. I think the stress of that has my tummy upset often."

"You know you could hire a tutor to help you out, Asia. I'm sure with extra help you could pass those classes," Mom said, trying to be helpful.

I knew Asia was a little worried about those classes. Her real worries were about us though. Our contract would be ending the very next day. We'd be free then. And as far as she knew, we still hadn't come up with a way to make the lies disappear so we could move forward as a real couple.

"I didn't think about that. Thanks." Asia smiled at my mother then looked up at me. "Maybe I should see about that then. In the next day or so, I'll do that. Remind me, would you?"

With a nod, I pulled her close, leaning my chin on top of her head. "I'll do that for you. No need to worry so much, Asia."

My father shifted in the seat. "You two need to understand one thing. Worry never solved anything. It's a wasteful emotion. Better to figure out what you can do to fix things, rather than worry about them. You have a problem, do something about it. Don't just worry and accomplish nothing but making yourself sick."

Dad was right, but Dad didn't know everything. Asia and I had a mountain of things to worry about. And what was worse, each and every way there was to fix it would cost both of us some kind of mental anguish.

At least with my idea, we'd both be hurt, but Asia would come out with her dignity intact. Only I'd be despised. A thing I wasn't looking forward to, but it had to be done.

"You're right, Dad. Worry has never solved a thing. Action will be taken so Asia can stop worrying."

Dad gave a nod of approval. "See to that, son. And I talked to Angie in human resources. Now, she told me that you've yet to go in and fill out the paperwork to put your wife on the insurance plans. Why is that? You've had nothing but time to get that done. You're going to start working with me in just a couple of weeks to learn the CEO role. You'll be very busy then. Best to get that out of the way before then."

"I'll get down there, Dad. It may seem like I've been free as a bird, but Asia and I have been doing all sorts of things."

Asia nodded. "We've been going and going. It seems like we hardly ever just sit around. But we should take the next couple of weeks and do just that. We both have work and school looming ahead of us."

I wondered if Asia would be too devastated to go back to school after I left her. I wondered how my parents would react to my going back to Los Angeles and picking up where I left off. Dad would have to maintain his role as CEO. I'd be deemed unworthy, and frankly, I didn't want to be in New York where I might run into Asia or her family.

It'd be best for me to be far away from them all. I knew my parents would get over things, eventually. But I doubted Asia ever would. Not entirely. She wouldn't die or anything, but there'd be a part of her that would remain broken forever. She trusted me. It was bound to leave a deep scar.

My leaving would leave its mark on me too. I'd never love anyone the way I loved Asia. I knew that. I'd never done anything so selfless in my life. I knew our love was true. If it wasn't, I'd feel just fine letting everyone think bad things about Asia.

I couldn't let that happen though.

"Oh, before I forget," Mom added. "The Petersons are having a dinner party next week. They asked me to extend the invitation to you two."

"Tell them, thank you, but we can't go."

Asia turned her head to look at me. "Don't say no on my account. I'm game, Jett."

I kissed her on the tip of her nose. "I'm not. I'm not a dinner party kind of guy."

"But, Jett, you should become one." Dad poured himself a glass of Scotch and gestured to me with the bottle. "Would either of you like a drink?"

"None for me thanks," came Asia's quick reply.

"I don't want one, either."

He put the bottle back into the rack of the small bar that held a dozen different types of alcohol. "Jett, you'll have to be more social once you become CEO. You'll be expected to attend charity events and dinners, all kinds of things. It's a big deal, you know."

Nodding, I thought about all that. My father had been doing all that stuff, along with his real job as CEO. I knew he was tired and needed me to step in a relieve him of that heavy burden.

My leaving would hurt him a lot too. He'd be left to keep up with the furious work pace and schedule. He deserved some rest after working like a slave to build something out of nothing.

When would the guilt stop piling up on me?

There was no right thing to do. No matter which way I looked, I would hurt people. I'd never been in a tougher spot. Admitting to myself that I brought this all down on myself did nothing to make me feel any better about things.

After all, what did knowing the facts and facing them do to end the never ending guilt?

I felt lost. Alone. Depressed.

And I had no one to blame but myself. Would I ever get things right?

I'd lived pretty much guilt free up until the beginning of summer when I fucked things up so well. Now it seemed I'd live the rest of my life with guilt.

I had to wonder if it would become something that didn't feel so horrible after a few years went by. But knew I was fooling myself. It would always feel terrible. But at least I was setting Asia free from it. Free from the lies, free from the guilt of telling her family a giant lie. At least she'd feel better. That was all I could care about. Asia, and how to make her feel better.

## 42

## ASIA

One minute I felt fine, the next my gut was twisting, and I was reaching for the door handle. "Tell the driver to wait at this red light." Opening the door, I hurled as Jett held onto me so I wouldn't fall out of the car.

"Baby!"

"Oh, my!" his mother shouted.

With the contents of my stomach gone, I felt better, but the embarrassment hurt like hell. I closed the door as found Jett running a tissue over my mouth. "Did that just hit you out of nowhere, Asia?"

I nodded and tried to regain my composure. "We need to get you to see someone right away," his father said.

"No wonder you're losing weight if this is what's been happening." His mother wagged her finger at us both. "This isn't something that occurs from stress or nerves. I thought you meant you weren't eating very much. I didn't know you were throwing up. We're going straight to the nearest emergency room."

"I don't..."

She shook her head. "I don't care. We're going, and you're going to be seen by someone right now."

"But the dinner," I whined.

"I'll let them know we won't be coming. You're more important than some damn dinner, Asia," his mother was adamant.

Jett rubbed my back as he eyed me with concern. "We're taking you to the hospital. No back talk about it, Asia."

Resting my head on his shoulder, I admitted defeat and faced the reality that I was going to have to see a doctor about it. Maybe he'd prescribe me some kind of anti-anxiety meds, and I could be on my way.

I felt horrible for getting in the way of his cousin's matrimonial festivities. But the three people, who were watching me like a hawk, didn't look like they'd be swayed by a word I said.

Relinquishing the battle felt kind of great. It was out of my control. I'd be taken care of. I found my heart swelling with love for all three of them. I did matter to them all.

When we arrived at the emergency room, we found it was full. And my upset tummy wasn't the biggest emergency there. A man was holding a towel around his hand, and red was beginning to soak through it. A little old woman was sneezing, hacking, and looking as if death was hovering around her, waiting for her to take her final breath. And three babies were crying with how badly they felt.

No, mine wasn't nearly as bad as anyone else's seemed to be.

So, we sat and waited and waited. After two hours, I told Jett's parents they should leave and Jett too if he wanted. I could take a cab back to the hotel once I was done there.

"Hell, no, Asia!" Jett wasn't having any of that. "I'm not leaving you here. Mom, Dad, you two go. Enjoy the rest of the night with the family. Tell them we're sorry, but Asia is sick."

They got up, making room for a couple of people who'd been standing. "They need the space in here anyway." His mother hugged me. "You call us when you find out what's wrong, Asia. We love you, dear."

Her words tugged at my heart. "I love you too. I'll let you know when I know something."

They left, and Jett looked at me. "She told you that she loved you, Asia."

"Yeah, I know. That was sweet of her." I took his hand and held it tightly. "I wasn't lying when I told her I love her too. I do. Your parents are great."

He nodded but looked a bit upset. I figured it was because of the falseness of our situation. But our love was real. We had to figure out a way to make things right. And soon.

"Asia Jones?" a nurse came out of a side door, looking over the crowd.

"That's me." I raised my hand and got up to go to her with Jett right at my side.

"Oh, good." She looked at Jett. "Are you related to her?"

He shook his head. "No."

"Then you'll have to wait here for her. No one except immediate family is allowed back. It's hospital policy. Sorry."

As she took my hand and pulled me inside, I looked over my shoulder at him and saw the frown that covered his handsome face. "Don't worry, Jett. I'll make this as fast as I can."

The door shut before he could say a word and I felt my stomach clench. The nurse took me to a large room with six curtain covered areas. "This is you, over here. Your admission paper says you've been throwing up. Is that correct?"

"It is." She handed me a gown and a small cup with a lid on it. "Go into the bathroom that's directly across the hallway." She took a Sharpie out of her pocket and handed it to me. "Write your full name and date of birth on the label of the cup. Fill it with urine, put the lid back on and leave it on the counter. Then take everything off but your underclothes and put on the gown." She handed me a plastic bag. "Your clothes can go in this bag. Bring them back in here with you when you're done. Do you understand all of that?"

With a nod, I said, "Write my name, pee, undress. What's so hard about that?"

"You'd be surprised at how many forget one or more steps in that process, young lady." The nurse patted me on the back. "Get into bed and wait for the doctor after you get that done."

So, I headed out to deal with all of that and found myself getting nervous and wishing like hell that they would've let Jett come back with me. I got it all taken care of, then went to lie in the uncomfortable hospital bed. The plastic mattress crinkled as I climbed on the bed and pulled the thin blanket up to cover me.

A man in green scrubs came in after a long time and smiled at me. Extending his hand, he shook mine. “Hi there, Asia Jones. My name is Doctor Sheffield. Can you say that for me?”

“Doctor Sheffield?” I asked as I had no clue why he’d ask me such a thing.

“Yes, I wanted you to say it. You’ll want to remember that name.” He let my hand go and patted my back. “You see, I want to be the first person to congratulate you.”

“On?”

“On being pregnant. Now, do you get it? You’ll tell your child about the day you found out you had him or her in your tummy. Doctor Sheffield was the person to tell you that great news.” His smile was huge, and his teeth were gleaming white.

His face would forever be etched into my brain. Thin, lightly tanned skin with a few wrinkles, plum colored lips, blue eyes, and a deep laugh that made his round belly shake made up the man who changed my life forever.

“I’m pregnant?” I shook my head in disbelief. “I’m on the pill. How can that be?”

He picked up the folder with my admission paper in it. “It says here that you began oral birth control on June the first of this year.” He looked at me with a grin. “Did you use condoms when you had intercourse during the first thirty days, Miss Jones?”

“No. I wasn’t told to.” I began to get short of breath.

“Yes, I see. But you were given paperwork from the pharmacy that you must not have read. That paperwork would’ve told you that you needed to use another form of birth control for that amount of time. By the way, stop taking them. They’re not safe for the baby.”

“Okay. Damn. I didn’t read it. You’re right. Shit!” My head was swimming.

I was pregnant!

His hand clamped down on my shoulder. “Let me tell you something,

Miss Jones. Babies have surprised people forever. I know you're freaking out now. But believe me, you'll love that little surprise when he or she comes out into the world. Don't make any hasty decisions. And let the father know. Let him have the chance to do right by this baby. You didn't make it alone. Don't make any decisions about it alone, either."

"Yes, sir."

His finger touched my chin as I stared at the floor. "You're going to be okay. The vomiting comes with pregnancy. I want you to find yourself a good Obstetrician as soon as you can. Set up an appointment and work with them to make sure you have a healthy pregnancy."

"Yes, sir." I had to lie back. "I just need a minute to digest all of this."

"I know. It's a lot to handle. Stay as long as you need to. But remember that there's a room full of people who are waiting to be seen too." He chuckled and waved as he left me. "I wish you the best, young lady."

I was going to have Jett's baby.

What the hell was I supposed to do now?

A nurse pulled the curtain back and gave me a huge smile. "Well, well, well, we're having us a baby. Are you excited?"

I gulped. "I don't know."

"You and the daddy getting along?"

"Yeah." I hung my head. "He loves me. He wants a baby. It was me who had major plans that a baby will interrupt." I looked up at her. "I don't want him to ask me to marry him just because I'm pregnant."

What was I going to tell Jett?

## 43

# JETT

Impatient and sick of waiting around, I managed to sneak in through one of the doors when a nurse came out to call in a patient. I was leaning on the wall next to it, hoping for an opportunity.

Not one member of the medical staff stopped me as I went through first one long hallway with various people moaning, complaining about their pain, or screaming in pain.

It was like a war zone in there.

There were curtains drawn around every patient, making it impossible to find Asia in any of the large rooms that housed the ER patients. I was relying on hearing her voice to get me to her.

Down another hall I went, passing a nurse as she stepped into one of the rooms. I waited on the outside of the door to see if I could hear Asia.

I heard the nurse say, "Well, well, well, we're having us a baby. Are you excited?"

I stepped away, knowing she wasn't talking to Asia.

Then I stopped dead in my tracks as it was Asia that I heard, saying, "I don't know."

The nurse asked, "You and the daddy getting along?"

Asia's voice began to quiver. "Yeah. He loves me. He wants a baby. It was me who had major plans that a baby will interrupt." She paused then went on, "I don't want him to ask me to marry him just because I'm pregnant."

I fell back against the wall and tried not to scream. I was going to be a father!

It was exactly what I had wanted, and I was getting it. The only problem was that I had other plans now. I was leaving her. I was doing it for her own good.

How would leaving her and our baby ever do anyone any good?

I was left once more, not knowing what the hell I should do. But I sure as hell would let Asia know that I was happy about this baby and would make sure the child always knew it was loved.

Heading back into the waiting area, I decided I wanted to let Asia tell me the good news. Since she had the diagnosis, it shouldn't take much longer for her to be released.

Another half hour had passed before she came out. Knowing she wouldn't want an audience to hear our news, I waited until we got outside to ask, "So, what's up?"

She took out her cell. "I've got a virus. I'm calling a cab to come get us."

A virus?

"What kind of virus?" I couldn't believe she wasn't telling me news she knew I'd be ecstatic over. "And what kind of virus lasts a month long?"

"A pretty bad one." She held up her finger at me as she told the cab company where to pick us up at.

Pinching the bridge of my nose, I fought myself not to confront her. What was she thinking?

Okay, I got it. She didn't want me to ask her to marry me just because we got ourselves preggo. I understood that. But I deserved to know about the baby.

Didn't I?

We both were quiet. The cab came, picked us up, took us to the hotel. Still, we were quiet. We went up to our room, got undressed, got into bed. Still, we were quiet.

I rolled over to look at her. "I love you, Asia."

She closed her eyes as she lay on her back. "I love you too, Jett."

But did she really?

How could she say those words to me?

She wouldn't admit to being pregnant. So how in the hell could she say she loved me?

Unless she didn't.

Maybe it had all been an act after all.

Lifting my head, resting it on my hand, I said, "The contract is over, Asia. The wedding is over. That was the last function I needed a fake wife for and the last day of the Dom/sub contract. Being that it's midnight, you're officially released as my sub. You can do as you want to now."

She didn't even bother opening her eyes. "All I really want to do is sleep, Jett."

All I really wanted was to hear her tell me about our baby!

"So what did they give you for this virus you have?"

"Some pills."

"Where are these pills?"

"I have to go pick them up at the pharmacy tomorrow." She finally opened her eyes to look at me as I hovered over her. "What are you doing?"

"Asia, are you realizing that you're rich now? You have a home of your own. A new car. And the money that I put in Escrow at The Dungeon of Decorum will be transferred to your bank tomorrow morning." I watched her eyes as they darted back and forth.

"Wow. You're right. I am a rich girl now."

"If you were giving me what I wanted just because you were my sub, you can be honest with me now. You're no longer my sub, Asia."

Her eyes went wide as she rolled out of bed and hauled ass to the bathroom, slamming the door behind her.

I was left without an answer. But I had a gut feeling it was going to be one that just might break my heart.

It hit me hard that Asia might not be telling me about the baby because she was thinking about getting rid of it.

Would I just stand back and allow that to happen?

I sure as hell wouldn't let that happen!

If Asia had been faking all this time, then I could let her go, but I wasn't about to let go of the baby. She'd be in for a fight if that was her plan. But I really couldn't see her thinking that way.

Asia had a good heart. Her morals ran deep. It was me who made her lie. If it hadn't been for me, she'd never have done one bad thing. No, she couldn't be thinking about getting rid of our baby.

But she might be thinking about ending things with me and having the baby on her own. Would I allow that?

I didn't want to. But I didn't know what to do about any of it.

How in the hell did so many things come to pass that I had no idea how to handle?

I wasn't a stupid man. But damn it, I was feeling pretty fucking stupid. My world was a lie. And I was afraid those lies were about to come crashing down on me.

Was I helpless to stop it? Could I change it all?

I had big decisions to make and not a lot of time to do that in. Getting up, I went to the bathroom door. The water was running in the bathtub. Then it went off and I heard Asia, "Little baby, I want you to know that I love you and I love your daddy too. But we've made up something and that lie is looming over us like a deadly shadow. If things were different, I'd be celebrating your creation with your daddy. But things are hard right now. Harder than I hope you ever have to live through. I know if I tell your daddy about you, he'll ask me to marry him. And I want to marry him. Just not over being pregnant. But there's also the fact that the lies will always hang over us if we stay together. Baby, I don't know what we can do to fix it all. But no matter what we do, always know that we both love you."

Falling against the wall, I held my head in my hands. I knew what I had to do. I had to make things right. Not only for myself and Asia, but for our baby too.

So I put my clothes on, and left.

# 44

# ASIA

After a long bath that did little to ease my mind, I went into the bedroom. The blankets were thrown back, the light was on, and Jett was nowhere to be found.

My heart began to race as I searched frantically for him, calling out his name over and over. I even opened the door and shouted down the hallway.

But he wasn't there.

He was gone!

And I was all alone.

Shaking, I went to get my cell and called him. His phone was off, it went straight to voicemail. I sat on the bed and searched my mind for what we'd said to each other that would have him leaving me.

Then it hit me.

The contract was over!

He left me because it was over. He'd been acting the entire time.

But why?

He didn't have to pull some act on me. Or was that something he just did? Did Jett Simmons hire subs to play out some weird fantasy love story with him, then leave them?

Had it all been a lie?

One lie on top of another one. And I was left with a baby inside me that belonged to a man who had it in him to do such a heinous thing. Jett could've been honest with me. He could've told me that was what his fantasy was. I'd have played along.

But I would've guarded my heart all the while. I bet he counted on that happening. I bet that's why he didn't tell me what his real fantasy was. He wanted a fake wife to avoid being set up. He wanted a sub to do it so he could live out a love fantasy. But it was all over now.

I was a thing of the past he could move on from.

My heart hurt like it would never mend. I laid on the bed as it all soaked in. It wasn't in Jett, to be honest. I knew that then. It had all been a fantasy to him. Never real, never lasting, never going to have my happy ending.

Left with a baby, a constant reminder of how I was duped, I'd live in the house he gave me, drive the car he bought for me, and live off the money he paid for me.

It was my own fault. I sold myself to the man for the period of three months. I signed a contract that said it would all end with no arguments what-so-ever. Jett was within his rights to leave me alone without one word.

But I wasn't prepared for that at all. And I'd fucked up by not letting him know that I had his child inside of me. No matter what he actually felt about me, he might love the baby we created together. He had a right to know. But I was bound by that contract not to attempt to contact him once it was over. I could lose the money that would be moved to my bank account the next day if I did that.

I needed money now. I had a baby coming. I couldn't afford to bother him with some news about a baby. I was supposed to be on birth control. I was pretty fucking sure that getting pregnant could be grounds for the money to be taken away from me.

I was going to be alone to have the baby, but I'd have what I'd earned. I gave that man more of me than I knew I could. I earned everything I got from him. Every last thing and every last cent.

Tears burst from my eyes as my body ached. I'd never feel his weight on me again. I'd never feel his warm breath as it tickled the back of my neck as I woke up each morning. The soft way he'd caress my body was over.

I'd never love anyone the way I loved him. If I could ever bring myself to fall in love again. A thing I didn't think I could do. It just fucking hurt so badly.

Sobbing into my pillow, I just wanted to leave the hotel and go home. Home to my family, not home to where I'd only see Jett in every corner. How was I going to live in that home?

How was I going to drive a car that reminded me of him? How was I going to look at a child that always reminded me of him? The man I once loved with more than I knew I had in me?

I was doomed.

Destroyed.

And desperately trying to hang onto my sanity.

Sleep wouldn't find me, I was sure of that. I'd be left awake in my torment. No peace would find me that night or ever. I was sure of that.

But eventually, the tears slowed and exhaustion took me over. Darkness came in at me from all sides, and I slept. Even in my sleep, dread filled my dreams.

Would I ever be the same again?

When morning light penetrated the window, I opened my eyes. Immediately, I looked to see if Jett had come back. All I found was the empty bed, and I'd wrapped my body around his pillow.

My stomach lurched, right on cue, sending me to the bathroom at breakneck speed. Once I stopped puking, I began to cry.

He was really gone!

It was really over, and I was really pregnant and all alone.

All I wanted to do was climb back into the bed, pull the blankets over my head, and go back to sleep. My dreams weren't peaceful or happy. But they weren't real, and even in my sleep, I knew that.

I was in reality. A place where it hurt me to be.

Slumping back to bed, I heard a knock on my door, and a piece of paper slid under it. The bill, I guessed.

I climbed back into bed and closed my burning swollen eyes. But the damn paper was nagging me to pick it up and see what it was. Getting up, I went to pick it up.

There was a message that had been left at the front desk by my parents. It said I needed to get up this morning and come to their house before I did anything else.

I bet they had some kind of a surprise for Jett and me. Well, it would be me who would surprise them with the news that Jett and I were through. And I had nothing ready to tell them about why that was.

I didn't want to go back to Harrison and face that huge empty house. And I didn't want to stay in the hotel Jett had left me in. Might as well go home, tell my parents he left me and I wasn't sure why. Must've been for another woman or something. But that I had a home, a car, and money. But I'd need to stay with them for a little while. Just until I got over it.

Somewhere in there, I'd have to add the part that I was now pregnant. Soon to be a single mother. But at least I had the means to take care of the baby. Going back to school would be out. I doubted my head would be right in two weeks anyway.

Gathering myself, I got ready to go to Queens to see my parents. Jett and I had only packed clothes for the next day. His were gone, he'd obviously put them on when he decided to leave me. But his tux was still there.

I folded it neatly and put it in the bag with the dress I'd worn to the wedding. It was then that I wondered if his closet would still be full of his things when I went back home. Would his car still be in the garage? Would his favorite coffee cup still be in the kitchen? His toiletries in the bathroom?

Maybe he'd get the maid to gather his things and send them to him in Los Angeles. I was sure he was going to go back there. Then my heart began to ache for his poor parents. He'd also duped his father, although I'm sure that was inadvertent, into thinking he'd be taking over his CEO job.

I knew I couldn't go to his parents and tell them about the baby, either. I had to leave them alone, per the contract, to avoid any contact with the Dom's family and friends after said contract was over.

Man, they'd love knowing about the baby, though. It didn't seem fair not to tell them about it. But I might have to give everything back if I did that.

My hands were tied. I had to follow the contract. Not for my sake but for the little guy who was living inside of me. The kid deserved at least some of what his father provided. I'd make sure to learn how to take care of the money he'd given me. I'd make it last, invest it, make it grow. I'd do it for our baby.

Dressed and ready to go, I headed to the lobby where the doorman hailed a cab for me and tipped his hat. "Have a lovely day."

That would be impossible. But I nodded. "You too." I got into the cab with my one bag, gave the driver the address of my parent's home and sat back. It was hard as hell not to cry as we pulled away from The Plaza Hotel. The place that would forever be etched into my brain as the place where my life, as I thought it would be, was ended.

Like all things, everything must end. But why did it have to end like this and leave me with a souvenir that would forever remind me of the man I lost?

## 45

# JETT

I had no choice but to do what I did.

Things had to be taken care of. There was just no other choice to make.

Sure it was hard. And sure I had to accept the fact that I'd hurt people. But it had to be done. There was just no other way to make things right.

Asia deserved to get to hold her head high. She was a good woman. And she was carrying my baby. I didn't want the lie to affect her any more than it already had. There was only the one way to fix it all.

Pain was part of that process. It had to be.

When lies get told, pain is always part of the process when you try to fix everything. Humility is learned. And so is the fact that lying comes with a high price.

Thankfully, the lies were over. And Asia would get to have her real life back. Not that make-believe one we were living. That life was over.

I had to say good riddance to that life. I was glad to have it behind me.

Who needs all that drama?

At least that's what I told myself as I drove my car away from our home that morning.

## 46

# ASIA

"Mom, Dad?" I pulled the screen door open and went into the home I'd grown up in.

"Mornin' baby girl." Mom came into the living room with an apron on. "Isn't this a lovely morning? Look at that sun. And can you smell the scent of autumn that's just around the corner? Oh, I can't wait for the first cold breeze to blow through our door."

She was so happy. Telling her would be hard. I didn't want to spoil her great mood. "You cooking breakfast?" I followed her into the kitchen after I dropped my bag by the door. It was then I realized that she hadn't asked me where Jett was.

But I wasn't about to say anything about it. Maybe she thought he'd come later. I didn't know, and I wasn't in the mood to spoil her mood.

"I have some wonderful things going on in here. Eggs, pancakes, sausage, bacon. Homemade biscuits are just about to come out of the oven, and the hash browns are nearly done too. If you pour yourself a cup of coffee or juice and take a seat, I'll have it all ready soon."

I went for a coffee cup then stopped. My sisters both cut out caffeine when they were pregnant. I should too, I thought. I went for the juice glasses and poured some bright orange juice into one.

The first sip was bitter, and I wrinkled my nose then took a seat. The heaping piles of food had me wondering if company was coming. Oh, I was not in the mood for company!

Before I could ask Mom about that, Dad came in and grabbed me by the shoulders as he kissed me on top of the head. "Well, look who's here. How's my baby girl this morning?"

Depressed. Dumped. Slightly deranged.

I didn't want to bring him down, either. Whatever the night and morning had done for my parents was great. I wasn't going to rain on their parade. "I'm doing well, Daddy."

"Good to hear." He made his way to Mom, snuggling her from behind then kissing her cheek. "Oh, honey this looks divine, and it smells like Heaven in here."

Was that it?

Had I died and gone to Heaven?

Nah, I still felt too bad for that to be the case.

The way my parents were acting had me rethinking telling them anything. I might just go back to Harrison and stay at home. I shouldn't bring them down with my tragic life.

I was the idiot who signed up to sell myself for the summer. A thing they didn't need to know about. And they sure as hell wouldn't feel sorry for me about how it all turned out.

I could already hear it. 'What the hell good did you think would come out of such a thing?' 'Are you insane?'

Nah, I'd keep things to myself. Eat their food and put a fake smile on my face. Then go home, see what Jett had taken and left then cry my eyes out.

That was my main plan anyway. It didn't matter where I stayed. I was just going to be crying anyway. No reason to burden anyone with my self-pity, self-loathing, and self-destruction.

A knock at the door signaled that my parents did indeed invite others to breakfast. "Come on in," Mom shouted as she took the biscuits out of the oven.

"Oh, my! It smells wonderful in here." Jett's parents stepped into the kitchen, and I went limp. His mother patted me on the back. "Good morning, dear. Point me toward the coffee, please."

Oh, crap!

I pointed at it then felt his father's hand on my back. "Isn't this a lovely day, Asia?"

"I guess."

Now, what was I going to do?

My parents were hobnobbing with Jett's!

He took the seat next to mine and turned to face me. "Your parents came up with a great idea. Sunday breakfasts at each other's houses."

Dad took a seat across from me. "Ours one week, theirs the next. We'll alternate. The best part is that we'll all get to spend time with our kids."

Fantastic!

Our families had already planned shit out. And I was left to ruin their breakfast and probably their lives too when I told them that Jett had left me.

It was getting pretty rough to figure out when to break it to them. Before the meal that my mother had worked so hard on, or after it? One way, they'd all lose their appetites and Mom's food would go to waste. The other way, they'd all have stomach aches.

I wanted to cry and got up, excusing myself for a moment. As I walked out of the room, I wondered why no one thought it was odd that Jett wasn't there too.

No one was saying a damn thing about his absence.

The screen creaked open, making me look up.

The sun shone behind the person, making them nothing more than a shadow. But it was a tall shadow. A muscular shadow. A familiar shadow. "Jett?"

He stepped into my parent's living room. A bouquet of flowers in one hand and a black box in the other. I was frozen.

What the hell was happening?

He got on one knee, holding out the small box. Behind me I heard the shuffling of chairs and then felt people at my back, looking on.

What the hell was he doing?

Our parents would want to know why the hell he was asking me to marry him when they thought we were already married.

"Asia Samantha Jones." He paused, and I walked closer to him. "I've come clean. I've told our parents how we met online at the dating site and I hired you to pretend to be my wife just to avoid the social problems that go along with being a single man. I told them how sorry I was that I made a moral young lady lie for me. I also told them that along the way I fell in love with you. I asked your father if I could have your hand in marriage and he said nothing would make him happier. So what do you say? Would you make me the happiest man in the whole world and become my wife, for real?" He opened the box, and a different engagement ring was inside of it. A bigger and better one than the one that was still on my finger.

I pulled the rings off my finger as my body shook and sobs held fast in my throat. "Jett, nothing would make me happier than becoming your real wife."

He put the flowers down and took the ring out of the box then slipped it on my finger. "Our lives start now. Our real lives." The weight of the ring felt better on my finger. Not one bit heavy. It felt like part of me. A part I never wanted to lose.

"Jett, I want to tell you something."

He stood and pulled me into his arms. "What would you like to tell me?"

I wanted him to be the first to know. I pulled him to me and whispered, "I'm pregnant."

His eyes glistened as he took my face in his hands. "You've made me happier today than I knew was possible, Asia." He kissed me, sweetly then looked at our parents as he wrapped me in his strong arms. "More great news. Asia just told me that we're having a baby!"

Suddenly, we were in the middle of a giant group hug as everyone shouted their congratulations and I cried with relief and happiness.

He'd done it!

He'd made everything right. We wouldn't have to lie anymore. I felt light as a feather with that weight off me.

Things were going to be okay. We'd get married, have our baby, and hopefully live our lives truthfully forever. I sure as hell was never going to lie about a damn thing again!

Jett rocked me in his arms when our parents backed off. They all went back into the kitchen to give us a moment of privacy. "Asia, I'm sorry that I left you alone. I'm sure you thought it was over."

Looking up at him, I pounding my fists against his chest. "Jett, you scared the shit out of me! I cried and cried until I fell asleep then I woke up and cried some more. I was devastated. Why didn't you just tell me what you were going to do?"

"Because you'd have demanded to come with me and take half the blame. I wanted to take all the blame. It was mine to take. And I didn't know how any of our parents would take that news. If your parents were super pissed, I didn't want any of their anger taken out on you. That's why I left, turned off my cell so you couldn't call me. I knew the sound of your voice would make it hard for me to go through with it. But I bit the bullet and told the truth and righted all the wrongs."

My heart was swelling with love for the man. He'd been so selfless. I'd never felt more pride in anyone before. I kissed him as I ran my arms around him. "Jett, I love you more than life, itself. I promise I'll be the best wife I can be. And I'll be the best mother to your child that I can be. What you did proves to me that you are a man I can rely on and be proud to call my husband."

His smile was priceless. "I'll try my best to be what you need in a husband. And I'll be the best father to our child that I can be. You never have to worry about a thing, I've got you, baby. Now let's go get some breakfast. I'm starving."

With a chuckle, he put his arm around my shoulders and led me to where our parents sat, waiting for us to join them at the first, every Sunday breakfast. It would be a tradition that would go on and on. As would our long and happy, real marriage.

# 47

# JETT

I couldn't wait to make Asia mine. We got on a private jet and headed to Vegas with our parents right there with us. I had her sisters and their families flown in too.

Asia would get the wedding she wanted!

We all spent a week there, preparing the perfect wedding for the love of my life. All the clothes had been bought. The flowers were picked out, and the small church was decorated lavishly. A reception in a private dining area of Asia's favorite restaurant was scheduled. She was getting her dream wedding. And sharing it all with our families made it that much more special.

The day of the wedding grew hectic, even though the plans had been made extremely well. I suppose that's just how weddings go. Things have to go wrong, or they'd be no fun!

Spring's baby spit up on her dress. My father, trying to help, took the baby from her and little Ray spit up on his suit too. Mom thought she was dabbing club soda on the spot on Dad's suit, but it turned out to be cola, staining it even more.

Asia was puking a lot, slowing things down. All I wanted to do was get the nuptials over so I could take my real wife to our room and make love to her as a real married couple.

Finally, the time came. Asia was ready. The music started, and there stood my gorgeous fiancée at the back of the room. Her white dress billowed out, making her look like the angel I thought her to be.

With slow steps, she came to me. I lifted her veil to find tears glistening in her pretty eyes. "Nice to see you, Miss Jones."

"Glad you could meet me here today, Mr. Simmons." She smiled at me, making my knees go weak.

We held hands and faced the pastor who got us to repeat things he said, and in the end, we kissed as man and wife.

The sensations that were running through me, I'd never experienced before. I was someone's husband. And not too far into the future, I'd be someone's father. Life was real for me then.

The reception was lovely and went on far too long. All I could think about was getting my wife up to our room.

When I could take it no longer, I swept her away from our families and took her up to our room. She looked at me with wide eyes as I rid her of the billowy dress. "We're really married, Jett."

"We are." I pulled the dress off her shoulders, letting it fall into a heap at her feet. Then held her hand, helping her to step out of the pile of material.

She pushed the jacket of my tux off my shoulders then unbuttoned my shirt. Her hands moved over my chest as she pushed it off me. I grabbed her by the wrists as her hands moved over my heart. "You feel that?"

She nodded. "It's pounding."

"Because it's full of love for you and our baby." I pulled her hands up and kissed them. "I'm complete now. I didn't know how great it would feel. It's indescribably pleasant."

I turned her around to take her bra off then pulled her back to me, taking her breasts in my hands. She reached back to undo my pants, and they fell to the floor. I stepped out of my shoes, and she stepped out of hers then we made our way to the bed. Quickly, we got rid of the rest of the clothing that was on us and climbed onto the large soft bed.

She lay on her back, gazing up at me as I stroked her cheek. "This time it's for real. I feel just like I did on our first night together."

"Me too." I leaned over and kissed her. Our tongues ran around together, playfully.

My hands roamed over her body as our kiss grew with passion. My cock was pulsing with desire, and I couldn't wait any longer. Moving my body to cover hers, I pressed my cock into her hot canal. Moans filled the air as we became one.

I had no idea it would feel different. But it did. It was as if we were making love for the very first time. I felt every little thing about her. The way her hips curved as I pressed against them. The way her breasts heaved as my chest squished them.

Watching her face as I made love to her, I saw a glow about her that I'd never seen before. My wife had a glow about her. My wife was in love with me. My wife had made me a very happy man.

I trailed my fingers over her shoulder, down her arm and clasped my hand with hers, pulling it up, holding it down. Then I did the same with the other, pinning her to the bed. "How powerful you make me feel."

She smiled and arched up to meet my thrusts. "You make me feel that way too."

I rolled over, sitting her on top of me. "I'm glad you feel that way too. I want to be the man who supports you, takes care of you, nourishes your soul."

"You are that." She ran her hands over my abs as she licked her lips. She was riding me at the speed she knew I liked, then she leaned over and kissed me.

We were married, and life was finally going to be just fine. The problems were behind us, and everything ahead looked sunny. A man couldn't ask for more than that.

## 48

## ASIA

I looked down at the man who was now my very real husband and smiled as I moved my body up and down his girth. There was a difference with how sex with him felt. It was better.

I had no idea it could get any better, but it had.

Steadily, I moved my body to stroke him as we looked into each other's eyes. It was real, and I was in a state of pure bliss.

Jett smiled and rolled us over, pinning me to the bed as he revved up the pace. I wrapped my legs around him, loving how much deeper he could go into me.

All the sweetness was moving to the back as the animal lust we had between us took over. He pounded me furiously as I moaned with how insanely good it all felt.

I raked my nails across his back, as he bit my neck. That was all it took to drive me over the edge, and I came like crazy. He held back, not ready to let it end. "Oh, baby. Yeah!"

Panting, I groaned as he kept going, making the orgasm go on and on. It finally ebbed enough that it wasn't driving me crazy. Jett smiled at me as he moved back. "On your knees."

I scrambled to get on them, eager to feel him back inside of me. He slammed into me and gave me a hard smack on the ass. Then he pushed my shoulders to the bed and held my waist as he made thrusts so hard, he grunted with each one.

With him going that deep and hard, it took no time to send me into a trail of orgasms that exploded inside me like firecrackers. One after the other hit me until I was quivering and moaning constantly with arousal.

Jett wasn't about to let it all end anytime soon. I realized that when he pulled out of me, turned me over and lifted me up. He put my legs over his shoulders, and I clung to his hair as he ate me out.

Lifting me up and down, he used his tongue to fuck me. I was screaming with desire. He couldn't seem to get enough of me. And I was overjoyed for that.

Picking me up higher, he moved his attention to my clit, using his lips to manipulate it as he continued to lift me up and down. I was screaming with another intense orgasm soon, and he put me down on the edge of the bed and rammed his cock into me, leaving it still as I pulsed all around it.

He stood there with his eyes closed as he took it all in. I watched a vein in his neck pulse with each rapid heartbeat then he began to move. Slowly at first, then he went faster, harder, and his eyes opened. "You belong to me, Asia. My cock is the only one that will ever be inside of you."

"Yes!" I was elated with how brazen he was.

"Only my seed will ever grow inside of you." He slammed into me hard over and over as I quivered with desire.

"Yes!"

I was his. I couldn't imagine being with another man. He owned me. Jett Simmons was my husband, and my heart would forever be his. And so would my body.

Taking me by the waist, he held me as he thrust his hard cock into me until I came again and he couldn't hold back any longer. He burst into me with a heat I found amazing. Then he stood there, perfectly still as his cock jerked inside of me.

It took a long time for our bodies to stop the pulsing and pulling from the strong orgasms. Then he moved me up onto the bed and placed my head gently on a pillow and went to get something to clean me up a bit.

I caught my breath as I closed my eyes and reveled in the afterglow. Then a cool cloth was running over my heated areas down south as my husband cleaned me all up. He left one small kiss on my clit before he came up to lie next to me. “Hey, you.” His lips met mine for only a second.

I ran my hand over her cheek. “Hey, you.”

“It’s real, Asia. You and I are a couple. A married couple. A real married couple.” He smiled. “Does that make you as happy as it makes me?”

I nodded. “It does. I didn’t know it could get any better, but somehow it is so much better.”

“For me too.” He kissed me again. “Knowing you’re really mine does something to me. It fills me with some crazy emotion. Love isn’t big enough to describe it. It’s like you’re a part of me now. A real part. Like if I lost you, it’d be like losing a piece of my actual body. Don’t ever make me lose you, baby. Promise me that. Promise me that we’ll always work things out. No matter what. Nothing will be too big that we can’t get over it or through it.”

To agree to that was easy. I wanted that security too. “Jett, I will never walk away from you. And if you try to walk away from me, you can bet your sweet ass that I’ll find a rope to tie you up with, I'll make you stay, and work with you until we’re both happy again. Because you’re that important to me. Losing you would be like losing part of my soul. We can get through anything. We’re a team.”

He shook his head and kissed me again. “We’re more than a team, baby. We’re one and the same. You and I are one, forever and always. And I’ll do everything in my power to keep your sweet ass happy.”

“Me too.” I smiled and raised my head to kiss him.

We’d done it. We’d made it all real.

We’d found our happily ever after…

**The End**

# ABOUT THE AUTHOR

Mrs. Love writes about smart, sexy women and the hot alpha billionaires who love them. She has found her own happily ever after with her dream husband and adorable 6 and 2 year old kids.
Currently, Michelle is hard at work on the next book in the series, and trying to stay off the Internet.
"Thank you for supporting an indie author. Anything you can do, whether it be writing a review, or even simply telling a fellow reader that you enjoyed this. Thanks

Facebook
facebook.com/HotAndSteamyRomance

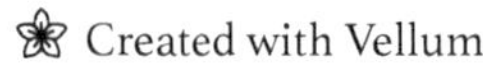
Created with Vellum

Lightning Source UK Ltd.
Milton Keynes UK
UKHW022145210622
404772UK00003B/74